Also by Dawn Klehr

The Cutting Room Floor

If
You
Wrong
Us

Dawn Klehr

If You Wrong Us

We all fall. Eventually.

flux
Woodbury, Minnesota

First Edition
First Printing, 2015

Book design by Bob Gaul
Cover design by Lisa Novak

Flux, an imprint of Llewellyn Worldwide Ltd.

Library of Congress Cataloging-in-Publication Data (Pending)
978-0-7387-4599-2

Flux
Llewellyn Worldwide Ltd.
2143 Wooddale Drive
Woodbury, MN 55125-2989
www.fluxnow.com

Printed in the United States of America

For my family
Oh, the things I'd do for you …

Acknowledgments

To say that bringing this book into the world was difficult would be like saying Becca Waters is a just a tad bit troubled. Writing dark books is tough, draining, scary. At times I'd think, should I really write such a thing? And maybe, even more importantly, I'd wonder, should people read such a thing? But then I finish, and it's ... cathartic. I feel like I've learned something, that I've grown. I feel like I better understand the people or places or situations that frighten me. I feel strong. I hope readers feel the same way.

Though I have to say, with the dark you must also have the light. I'm so lucky I do!

First, middle, and last, I'd like to thank my husband, Lance, who watched me sleep on the couch for two months surrounded by books, movies, music, art, and anything else I could use for inspiration as I finished this damn thing! He bravely endures the crazy when I'm preoccupied with my work and, amazingly, never asks me why I do it. He also keeps the candy bowl on my desk full, the kiddo entertained, and the household running, and I simply adore him for it.

To my son: who, on the other hand, constantly begs me to please "just quit writing," thank you for putting up with it, buddy. And for making me take breaks, giving me plot ideas, and reading with me every single night before bed. It's the very best part of my day.

I'd also like to thank Brian Farrey-Latz and Jessica Sinsheimer for their enthusiasm for my wicked characters and for getting scared in all the right places. I appreciate all that you do.

Boatloads of gratitude to Sandy Sullivan, who was so patient and kind as we got to the homestretch, and who allowed me to make edits and additions up until the very last minute. She is a dream to work with. Also to the Flux team dedicated to bringing all kinds of books to young readers, particularly the editorial, design, sales, marketing, and publicity departments.

Huge hugs go out to my writer pals who share their talent and support in so many ways. To Sara Biren, who lovingly calls me "sicko" when I share my story ideas and who always comes to the rescue when I send out the S.O.S. To Rhonda Helms, for helping me tighten up my originally scattered opening and for providing the encouragement I needed to keep going. Also to the MNYA writers, who read so many different versions of this story and pretended never to get bored—and especially to Liz and Nikki, who helped come up with the idea for Hush.

As strange as it sounds, this story is about family, especially those who always have your back. Mine always does and I love them to pieces! *And if you wrong us…*

To admit wanting revenge is to admit
you have been crushed and need to be rebuilt.
—Laura Blumenfeld,
Revenge: A Story of Hope

In revenge and in love woman is
more barbaric than man is.
—Friedrich Nietzsche,
Beyond Good and Evil

The Elements of a Crime

According to criminal law—a subject I've had to become very familiar with as of late—four elements of a crime must be proven beyond a reasonable doubt to convict a defendant. Cue the *Law and Order*, dun dun.

Of course, I have them memorized.

- **Element #1:** Mental state. Was the criminal act voluntary or purposeful?

- **Element #2:** Conduct. Did a criminal act or an unlawful omission of an act occur?

- **Element #3:** Concurrence. Did the intent and criminal act occur at the same time?

- **Element #4:** Causation. Did the intent and conduct of the accused lead to the crime?

All of this complex legal speak can really be broken down into just two simple factors—a guilty mind and a guilty act. Without these elements, a case can unravel. A case like mine. And should I ever get caught, it's something I'm banking on.

After all, it's a numbers game.

1

Last night, as I drifted off to sleep, I pretended I was innocent.

It wasn't that hard to do there in my bed, under the gritty sheets and stale bedspread—a painful reminder that made this illusion a necessity. When she was alive, I never even noticed clean bedding. I never worried if there was enough food in the cupboard, or shampoo in the shower. I didn't have to. But now, I no longer take these things for granted.

Burrowing farther into my rank covers, I shut out the blue flicker of light that seeped in from the living-room TV and ignored the dull voices that hummed behind the closed doors. Then I imagined my parents in the next room, spooning each other and giggling their way into a blissful sleep (something I used to find repulsive, but now desperately miss), dreaming of whatever it is happy parents dream of. I fantasized about spending my days playing baseball and planning for college instead of plotting, stalking, and trading in on all my favors to get my hands on a gun. I conjured up a guilt-free mind, a stable home, and a nice girlfriend who was sweet and simple.

Then I woke up and the truth smacked me in the face.

Today's the day. Not that anyone would know. This morning, I went through the same routine I have since school started: got dressed, brushed my teeth, fixed my hair right, made hardboiled eggs—three for me, one for Cassie—checked in on Dad to see if he wanted any even though the answer was always no. I finished the math homework I was too tired to do the night before and caught a ride to school. Nothing out of the ordinary.

By second period, it's more of the same, and things are moving just as smooth as a flat-seamed baseball. I'm one of the first to take my seat. Usually, it's a race to beat the bell. But for Mrs. Skye? I haul ass ... because I need to watch.

Sometimes I wonder just how far back in time I'd need to go to make my pathetic fantasy a reality. It'd definitely have to be life before Becca. And before the accident. But would that be far enough? I'm in this impossible situation because I'm self-centered, and needy, and weak. So I'd have to go way back in time, before I became all these things, to prevent the coming attractions. To undo all the things I have in store for the guy sitting behind me.

His breath is warm—almost wet—on the back of my neck as he leans over his desk waiting for class to begin. A prickly sensation shoots down my spine and it takes everything I have not to turn around and backhand him. Dude is completely encroaching on my personal space, but I know I can't bring any attention to myself.

Revenge, I've come to learn, is not impulsive, or reactionary, or blind. It's calculating, patient, and observant. And if it's going to work, the timing must be perfect. Just like in baseball. Swing too early, risk a pop-up. Swing too late, risk a strike.

I can't risk a thing today, so I grit my teeth and suffer through it as he sits behind me, ready to snuggle in for his daily nap. I slide forward in my tiny chair so I can pretend he's not back there. So I can pretend the asshole doesn't exist. Within seconds, he drops his head to the desk. His breathing slows and deepens, creating a nasally little tune before he's out. I envy him that. He dozes off at this time every day like clockwork—most likely because he was up half the night playing some zombie apocalypse bullshit video game. But in fifty minutes, he will somehow wake just as Mrs. Skye wraps up one of her highly sanitized lessons in U.S. History.

This is how Travis Kent spends his mornings.

It was so much better when I didn't know about him. Now I can't get his face out of my head. When I go to bed at night? Travis Kent. When I wake up in the morning? Travis Kent. Even when I'm with my girlfriend ... Travis Kent.

Shudder.

But in less than twenty-four hours, that will all change. Travis Kent will be extracted from my life forever.

I shift around in my seat, trying to get comfortable. It's impossible because I'm stuffed into this desk-and-chair combo—much like Rosie is, sitting next to me jammed into her two-sizes-too-small bedazzled jeans. It's tight and confining.

I don't know who designs the desks for high schools, but they need to seriously rethink the dollhouse dimensions. Though I shouldn't complain; at least we *have* a place to sit. Many of the classrooms don't. Ever since Roosevelt High School closed its doors two years ago, Central got most of the overflow—and that's exactly what it is. Our already-crowded school is now leaking students. The principal even had to extend the time between bells due to the gridlock in the corridors.

Apparently this is what happens when your city goes bankrupt: businesses and schools close their doors; unemployment goes up; the police force suffers massive cutbacks; people get desperate; crime rises.

It's every man for himself.

So I guess you could say I'll be doing everyone a favor by decreasing the headcount tonight.

These days, the only part of Detroit that doesn't look like a dystopian wasteland is Mexicantown—a place people used to wrinkle their noses at but were happy to visit on a Friday night for margaritas and enchiladas. Now, we're the ones holding the damn city together.

"Johnny Vega." Mrs. Skye's shrill voice echoes in the room. "What does Manifest Destiny mean?"

"Uh," I say, searching my brain for the question she just asked. "Manifest Destiny?"

I'm still not used to the whole student-teacher protocol. I never used to be the type of kid teachers called on in class. They would avoid me even more than they avoided the loner kids on the verge of going Columbine at any minute. Most teachers around here believe it's best to just let the dumb

5

jocks skate by—especially the dumb Mexican jocks. That's a double violation, after all.

But that was before Becca came into my life and before I started caring about school (and using words like "encroaching" and "dystopian"). Before I realized that there may be more to life than ball. Truth be told, I've always cared. I just didn't think school was my *thing*. But once I started showing an interest, teachers like Mrs. Skye ate it up.

She desperately wants to be that determined white teacher who makes a different for us poor minority folk—like that movie *Freedom Writers* or some shit.

Let's face it, I probably need it. This is one of the "basic" courses—in other words, for idiots, stoners, or slackers. Travis doesn't fit in; he's only here because he makes a habit of taking extended vacations.

"Yes, Mr. Vega." Skye interrupts my wandering thoughts. "Tell me what Manifest Destiny means to you."

It was a way for America to justify destroying the way of life for Mexicans and Native Americans and steal our land.

It's the first thought that comes into my head, but now—thankfully—I take a minute to think *before* I speak.

Mrs. Skye stares at me. Waiting. She flicks her pen against her thigh as she paces in front of the room. Yeah, she's impatient that I need a second to gather my thoughts, yet Travis is allowed to use the hour as naptime every day. I've come a long way in the last year, but the politics of high school is something I'll never get.

"Manifest Destiny is an idea or belief that Americans should expand across North America and promote democracy."

I alter my answer because I have the feeling our teacher was all for the expansion. With her immaculate clothes and shiny shoes, Mrs. Skye is the type to believe that anything is possible in our great country and to downplay the negative—even when the city is collapsing all around her.

"Good," she says, moving on. "Cody, was that a good or bad thing?"

And I'm back to tuning out again.

I'll need to find extra time to study the material for our test in two days. Not that it's difficult, obviously, but I've been checking out for the past week and I can't leave anything to chance. Becca says we can't have any hiccups; it has to be business as usual. For me, that means a decent grade on the test. Still, I find myself ignoring Mrs. Skye and staring out the window, watching the last of the falling leaves. I wonder if next year I'll be watching them from a college classroom or a jail cell.

It's completely impossible to concentrate, today of all days. I'm on edge. Teeth-grinding, stomach-churning, fingers-tingling edge. And here Travis sleeps, with no idea what he's in for. He'll go about his day as usual. Chemistry, study hall, lunch, gym, English, finishing with Spanish—a language he'll never master, by the way. The guy can't roll an *R* to save his life.

I know all of this because I've been watching him for almost ten months. Obsessing over him, really. Ever since Becca told me what happened and what he did. Ever since I said yes to her plan.

A pen drops on the floor and the desk behind me rattles. I don't have to stalk Travis to know he's a restless sleeper—it's pretty common knowledge in our class. Sometimes I wonder if it's guilt or bad dreams that affect his sleep in this way. Or is it simply because he spends too much time jacked up on oversized cans of Monster and Starbucks mochas (with extra whipped cream)?

Oh yeah, I've been watching his calorie intake as well. If I go through with tonight's festivities, I'll have to carry good ol' Trav a few blocks. I'm pretty strong, but Travis is surprisingly solid for a guy barely over five-five.

The fact that I know all of this is sick and wrong. I do know that; I'm not so far gone I don't understand the moral dilemma we're in. But I'm doing it for Becca ... and Mom.

Though I'm not sure Mom would've approved of Becca if she were still here. She always warned me about hanging out with the wrong crowd, bad influences, or *those people* who didn't help you meet your life's goals. *We can't let anything get in the way of your dreams, Johnny,* she would say. Funny how her threats always seemed to be disguised as motivation.

What Mom didn't know is that trouble is not always so obvious. Not when it comes in a pretty package like one Becca Waters. Long and lithe Becca, with her flowing red curls and angelic face. Trust me, she's enough to turn the strongest of men into drooling idiots. I had no idea what I was up against when she started tutoring me last year. She was so broken then, and my connection to her was almost immediate. What's that expression: *like recognizes like*? Well, we recognized each other all right, and it wasn't long after that I vowed to do whatever it took to put her back together again. Sadly, it's officially come to that.

After school, we'll wait while Travis meets up with his other gamer friends. They'll talk smack about leveling up and a bunch of crap only those fools understand. Of course, Becca gets it. She's tried explaining their little subculture to me, but I'm so not interested. Though I would love to see her kick some of these douche-canoes' asses, Becca prefers to use her mad skills IRL—which is exactly how she found out about Travis in the first place.

Tonight, Travis will go to the gaming tournament. After, his life will change forever.

So will mine. Everything I've worked for will be in jeopardy. My only hope is to pray I make it out of this shitstorm unscathed. But it won't be easy. To get out of it, I may have to leave Becca.

And I'm just not sure I can do that. No matter the cost. Right now, our plan is the only thing that makes sense. One action to right the wrong and give us a new life.

Like Mom always used to say, "Two birds, one stone, my love. Two birds, one stone."

2

ONE YEAR EARLIER
BECCA

"You make the rules," I told her.

They were four little words. Four very telling words that pretty much summed up my sixteen-year relationship with my twin sister, Brit. Four words that would play on an endless loop in my mind in the months that followed because they would become my final concession. And also the last words I said looking into her eyes—those green and almond-shaped pools of mystery that went all glossy when she was up to something.

She most definitely was.

That autumn day had started out like any other. I braided my hair in a long tail to keep it out of my face and dressed in a freshly starched pale blue button-down, khaki skirt, and Dad's tweed coat—the one he was wearing when he found out he'd been accepted to Princeton's graduate program. I considered it a uniform of sorts. Or armor, depending on the day. But that was a secret I'd never divulge.

"I swear to God, Bee," Brit said from her perch at the vanity table in our bedroom. "I'm going to burn that damn thing. What do you think—wearing that is going to bring you luck? Like it's some kind of good omand or something?"

"Omen," I corrected her, even though it still wasn't the right word. My twin was incredibly obtuse at times. Still, I always knew what she was trying to say. A fact that frightened me to my very core.

"Whatever." She dismissed me with a flip of her wrist. "Is that why you wear it? Hoping the good juju will rub off?"

"No," I snapped, insulted. I most certainly was not superstitious. Far from it—I didn't believe in luck. Most people got what they deserved based on their work ethic and decision-making capabilities. It was as simple as that. "I like the history of the coat. That's all. Plus, it's warm and goes with everything. Why do you find that so offensive?"

"Well, maybe I wouldn't"—Brit laughed—"*if* Dad ever *went* to Princeton. But since he got Mom knocked up and never made it to the Ivy League, I'd say anything you'd associate with that smelly coat is bunk. And it makes you look like a freak."

As if that ever bothered me before.

What Brit failed to understand is that while she had clout among the masses at our crowded and neglected high school, I also carried weight inside those walls. Albeit my status was strictly reserved for kids in the Accelerated Student Program (ASP)—a small group of students enrolled in specialized courses since we had already surpassed most mainstream classes, especially in math and science. It was the only group in school that really mattered, in my opinion. Because the tide would eventually turn, and the people my sister worked so hard to impress would all be answering to us in the future. So being called a freak was hardly a concern.

And that bothered the hell out of my sister.

Downstairs at the breakfast table, my mother's assessment of my wardrobe was in line with Brit's, but she at least faked it. Mom had once been a girl just like Brit and they had a bond I never quite understood.

"Morning, girls," Mom said without looking in my direction. "Don't you two look nice today." She ran her hand down my sister's long wavy hair, which was perfectly tousled to give the impression she was relaxed and carefree. In reality, it took Brit over an hour to make it look that way.

I ignored them like I usually did, sat at the table, and began reading my physics material for the following week. Dad peeked out from his newspaper—the archaic, paper variety—to give me his signature wink. The one that said, *we are superior to their kind.*

Brit slurped her coffee, staring at me over her cup as I ate my granola and continued to read. It was her way of telling me to hurry up. We had things to discuss before school—more like, she had orders to hand down. Orders I didn't want to hear. So I took my time, until she kicked me under the table.

I went to the refrigerator and grabbed the lunches (plural) that I'd made the night before. If I didn't, Brit would end up stealing half of mine, so I now made two. Lunch money was just the latest luxury to go in our slide toward the poverty line. Of course, Brit said, "It's okay, Dad. We can brownbag it. It's healthier anyway." Meanwhile, she was the one with her hands in his wallet—or pants pocket, or seat cushion, or dresser—slowly building up her beer funds for the weekend.

"Are you ready for tonight?" she asked when we got into my car. The car I'd paid for with my tutoring money. Not that she cared. The passenger side was full of dirt on the dashboard where she constantly propped her feet, and fingerprinted windows from her grimy digits drawing in the condensation. I'd given up on cleaning her side and strangely found comfort watching her sit there in her own filth each day.

"I'm ready," I told her, having already agreed to her plan to get rid of my secret boyfriend. A guy, she said, who wasn't worth shit.

"Just act normal." She reapplied her lip gloss. "It'll all be over soon enough."

My chest clenched a little at those words, but I pushed away the thought. She picked up on it, though. The next moment, she was leaning over the seat and I was trapped in one of her confining hugs.

I went limp on contact, like I usually do when anyone touches me unexpectedly.

I don't like to be touched that way. Unexpectedly. In certain situations, I can fake it. A hug for my aunt in greeting. A grateful handshake for a professor after a compelling lecture at an ASP event.

And sex. Then I don't mind it. After all, touching is the nature of the act. Even the unnecessary moves—the grabs and strokes and holding—make sense in the moment because they're leading up to something.

But an unwarranted hug, or brush of the leg, or squeeze of the arm?

No.

Just no.

That makes me queasy.

"It's for the best," my sister said in my ear after the unwarranted contact. "You know I've always got your back."

Brit loved exercising her self-appointed position as HBIC (Head Bitch in Charge). To me, she was simply HB. My sister was the type of person who got off on power, especially over boys. This latest situation I'd fallen into was her favorite type of problem to fix.

We'd argued about her plans, and I'd made a damn good case for her to just drop it, but in the end Brit prevailed. That was nothing new. She was going to pay him a visit after school. It was as good as done.

At first I wasn't worried, because I was prepared. To survive my childhood with Brit, I'd always had to be one step ahead of the game. This time was no different; I was ready.

Once we got to school, I parked at the far end of the lot, where the risk of a door ding was at its lowest. We walked to the side door of the building, where I immediately caught his stocky body against the wall, lurking in his normal spot. I tried to shake him off with a curt nod and pushed Brit inside the door to keep her from noticing. I would *not* be joining him today.

"Jesus, Becca," Brit said.

"Sorry." I kept shoving. "I'm going to be late for class."

"Nice try." She moved out of my reach. "We still have ten minutes."

"But I need to talk to my teacher before the bell."

"You have issues." She painted on her smile and waved to the clones as they shuffled by us. "Seriously, it's not the end of the world if you don't break the curve for every flippin' assignment."

I let it go because my distraction served its purpose and there was no point in engaging any longer. Wiping my sweaty palms on my skirt, I nodded. "You're right. I'm just nervous. We have a lot going on today."

She softened then. As much as Brit loved to give me grief, she loved to comfort me as well. Hugs and kind words; gentle pats on the back and teen-pageant smiles. I find it odd that there's such a fine line between love and hate. With my sister, that line was razor-thin.

"Don't worry," Brit said. "I've got this. Give me your keys. I have Kelser last period and can talk him into letting me out early. I'll get the car and meet you here right after the bell. Don't be late. Then I'll drop you at home and go take care of our little problem. Okay?"

"Yeah, okay," I said, handing her the keys. "You make the rules."

She twirled the key chain around her index finger and grinned. That was just the way she liked it.

3

JOHNNY

After the bell dismisses History class, Becca meets me in the hallway. My gut sinks when her eyes follow Travis as he walks out the door. A predator and its prey.

When she turns to look at me, however, her eyes warm and shine the brightest green. She tips her head to the side in greeting and her strawberry-colored hair falls haphazardly around her shoulders. Our tutoring relationship became a little more interesting six months ago, and we've been together ever since. But I still get mental around her. It doesn't help that I haven't seen her since yesterday.

Last night she was volunteering at the hospital, but the night before we went to the movies. Becca indulged me; she's not into movies. After, we had sex in her car. It sounds cheap, but it wasn't. I love—make that adore—the girl. Though she makes me completely crazy. The way she gives one minute—her time, her attention, her body—and then withholds it the next. It keeps me coming back for more, and has me agreeing to almost anything. When she's in my line of sight, everything but Becca blurs and goes fuzzy.

It does for her, too. I know it does, even if she won't admit it.

It's a chemical reaction, she'd say. She always has some sort of logical explanation for the illogical. Like when I told her I loved her for the first time and she said, "No you don't." She was absolutely serious.

"You're feeling a chemical reaction," she continued. "Though we may call it love, it's really only a reaction from the estrogen, testosterone, dopamine, norepinephrine, serotonin, and oxytocin in the body. That's what neuroscience tells us. Or the feelings could simply be from some biological need all humans have to pass along their genes. And I won't even go into the psychology of it all."

I just laughed. It was all I could do. Then I conducted my own chemical experiment, crushing my lips into hers, letting my body tell her how I felt.

That shut her up for a while.

"Hey, Beautiful Mind," I say now, crossing the hallway to her.

She rolls her eyes. She hates when I call her that, which is exactly why I still do it. Though I don't mean it in the John Nash schizophrenic way; I mean it in the brilliant mathematical way. I'm pretty convinced my girlfriend is a genius.

Johnny Vega—dating the school's valedictorian. Who would've thought?

I put my arm around Becca and pull her to my side. She's bony and her skin feels like ice. This is all taking a serious toll on her. I'm sure she didn't sleep last night either. It's been this way for weeks now. I just hope when it's all over, we can go back to normal. Whatever *that* might look like.

"Are you okay?" I whisper in her ear. She blinks and gives me a quick smile.

"I'm fine," she says as she squirms out of my arms.

And that's Becca. She pretends not to feel. She tries to be logical and clinical and cold. But she hurts. She hurts harder than anyone I know, and that's including my dad—who lost his other half too.

Last year, Becca lost her twin sister Brit in a car accident.

It was the same accident that took my mom; the accident that brought Becca to me. When we first started talking, I was in pretty rough shape. But Becca? She was worse. Her parents were making her go to Twinless Twins, a support group based on some specific twins-related psychology. It was about the saddest thing I'd ever heard. I've since discovered that psychology might actually be my *thing*, but it's Becca's nemesis. It's one of the sciences that she believes holds no weight. I can't imagine the kind of shit she pulled in that group, but know it couldn't've been good. I think she lasted three weeks. On her terms or theirs, I have no clue.

Becca looks up and those green eyes zero in on me. She knows I'm analyzing her. She doesn't like that, either. So she backs me up against the row of lockers and kisses me.

She brushes her lips across mine, slowly, gently. Her tongue slides along my bottom lip ever so slightly. And before I can run my hand up the back of her neck to hold her in place, she slips away.

It's one of her distraction techniques—one of the better ones. For someone who says she's never had a boyfriend, she knows what she's doing. I'm completely wrapped around her little finger.

Mr. Swanson walks by and clears his throat.

"Uh-oh," Becca whispers. "The Enforcer."

That's one of my girl's many—shall we say—quirks. She doesn't like to use people's names, other than mine, anyway. She prefers her self-designated titles: *The Enforcer, Pack Leader, Hall Monitor, Socio, Daddy Issues*. She likes to keep a nice healthy distance from anyone and everyone because, in her mind, it helps her stay in control.

For Travis Kent? Well, she refers to that asshole as *The Opponent*. I guess it's because she considers all of this some kind of fucked-up game.

Once I asked how she would label herself. *Broken Girl*, she answered.

I'd have to agree with that.

I pull Becca back to me, not willing to lose our connection so soon. My arms snake around her and my hands settle on the small of her back. I have to fight the urge to let them drop lower. Becca has no idea how hot she is, and *that* only makes her more appealing. I nestle into her neck, breathing in her clean, soapy scent.

For once, she lets me.

The two of us stand there in the hallway, wrapped up in each other, as the whole world continues to go on around us. Unaware of the pain that threatens to break us every day, or the strength we gain from it. Oblivious to our plan to make things right.

Tonight, everything has been arranged down to the minute. Yes, it's rash and cruel and twisted. But nobody will get hurt. And we need this, Becca and me. With each day that passes without Mom and Brit, we both die a little. Soon there'll be nothing left of either of us.

When I finally release her, Becca's eyes droop like they do every time she's worried. We're taking such a big risk tonight. It could be the end of everything, and I know she feels it too.

"Come on, Vega." She bumps my hip. "Pretend you're a gentleman and walk me to class."

I grab her hand, trying not to think about anything but this—walking with my girl in school. Just like any normal couple. We reach her class as the warning bell goes off, giving me two minutes to get to the other end of the building.

"Better get to class," I tell her. "I can't be late."

Becca nods. She knows this. We can't have any missteps.

"Okay, see you tonight."

"Here, take this," I add, shoving a granola bar into the chest pocket of her button-down shirt. "I like my women with a little meat on their bones."

Then I break into a run down the hall. And for the rest of the day I get lost in my head, mapping out every detail of tonight's plan.

Becca would call it proper planning.

The authorities would call it premeditation.

4

BECCA

On the drive home that day, music blared from my cheap car speakers and Brit bit at her lip. She gnawed and chewed at it until tiny translucent pieces of skin flaked off, leaving little speckles of blood in their wake. She was scheming.

She drove exactly twelve miles over the speed limit, leaving a residue of cake-batter-fragranced lotion on the steering wheel from her over-moisturized hands. I knew I'd eventually become nauseated by the scent.

While she was lost in her own thoughts, I turned the radio to NPR. It was another discussion about downfall of our great city, one that must have brought them high ratings because they went at it from all angles. People were all too happy to listen. We're peculiar creatures in that way—it's like sad, tragic, and depressing news gives us an excuse or reason why our lives are so disappointing. We can't get enough of it.

The story piqued my interest too, but for different reasons. It was all about crime. Apparently, if you wanted to get away with murder, Detroit was *the* place to do it. And according to the "expert" on the radio, the facts were indisputable. I only caught the last three of them:

- **Fact:** 91% of Detroit crimes go unsolved
- **Fact:** 70% of all murders go unsolved
- **Fact:** 40% of the area's streetlights are currently out of commission

In summary, Detroit was dark and dangerous. These were facts that would stay with me for quite some time, though I had no idea how important they'd become.

Brit and I didn't talk at all during the drive, though my sister still managed to reach for me when we came to the railroad tracks. We lifted our legs and slapped the roof of the car with our linked hands as we crossed. We'd done this a million times before.

It was for luck, according to Brit. Yet despite doing our little ritual all those times, we were the most doomed twosome you'd ever meet. There's no such thing as luck, just as I said.

Still, those were the moments I liked best with my sister. The quiet times when we didn't need to talk were when we said the most to each other. I'd always been terrified of my feelings. I rarely showed emotion. Not because I didn't feel, because I felt too much. My feelings were too intense, and I worried that if I chose to acknowledge them, they'd consume me whole. It was easier to push them down. They were for the weak, anyway. Over the years, I'd learned to manage my emotions, contain them. I'd learned to place logic and reasoning and control above all else.

Even above love. Or *especially* above love.

After pulling into our driveway, Brit quickly braided her hair and took off her makeup to look more like me. It worked. We were the epitome of identical; only our clothes and hairstyles set us apart. Once, a guy in my biology class asked if it was weird to look at my sister. He wanted to know if it was like looking in the mirror, if it was *freaky*. It wasn't. Actually, when I looked in the mirror, I saw her, not me. I never really saw me.

I got out of the car, and Brit gave me a little wave as she backed up. For some reason, I didn't return it.

After she left, I spent the first hour cleaning the house before our parents got home. Our house was the kind of place that screamed mediocrity. Dad's old books on the shelves, and Mom's tiny art collection hanging in the corner, complemented the old chipped desk that held a box of clipped coupons and credit card bills with mounting late fees. It was the kind of home that said, *I was on a path but was derailed, and now I've settled. I've given up and will do only the minimum necessary to survive.*

My parents had moved to this house, which sat on the border of Corktown and Mexicantown, from their tiny apartment in Ann Arbor—once they found out that their little *oops* was actually two little *oops*. This area of Detroit is an eccentric melting pot and my parents thought it would be "cool" to raise kids in the city, exposing us to culture before settling in the suburbs. This, of course, was before the city's bankruptcy.

As I dusted Mom's milk glass collection, I imagined Brit arriving at his house for the surprise of a lifetime. He'd tug on her braid and laugh, knowing it wasn't me—since I'd already told him about the switcheroo. She, in turn, would roll her eyes at him and look down her nose, disgusted to be in his presence.

He wouldn't like that.

His younger brother would be watching from the periphery, worried as Brit began to raise her voice.

That would make him even angrier.

It made me angry.

Made my hands hurt.

A loud shattering snapped me out of it. The sound: glass colliding with ceramic. The sight: blood dripping on the floor.

Lost in thought, I'd squeezed too hard and broken Mom's favorite vase. It fell to the floor, and tore up my hand more than you'd expect.

Funny, the blood didn't bother me. But the mess sure did.

I put things back in order and went to our bedroom to wait for my sister's return. Taking a deep breath, I tried to shake away the uneasiness swishing around inside. Then I found my favorite mechanical pencil (the Pentel Graph Gear 1000) and focused on the first problem of my Calc homework. AP Calc BC, to be precise. We were working on derivatives in class, and normally solving problems calmed me.

I enjoyed the entire process: propping my textbook on a stand at a 45-degree angle; placing the graph paper on the desk directly in front on me; rolling the pencil in my left hand. The way the hi-polymer lead smelled the moment it hit the crisp white graph paper was euphoric, as was the feeling of the brushed metallic barrel on my fingers. It was perfectly smooth and cool, contrasting with the warm cushioned rubber pads on the grip.

Brit always gave me a hard time about my obsession with pencils, but mathematicians are very particular about their writing tools. That was what I wanted to do with my life.

Calculus, the most important branch of mathematics in my view, is single-handedly the best subject in high school— if you're lucky enough to have the prerequisites required for the class.

I was.

I loved the way it built on every math principal I'd ever learned, the amazing proofs, the absolute logic. Calculus was a perfect world, and I was allowed access just by working the problems. Neat, clean, sensible.

Yet at the moment, it did nothing to soothe my nerves.

I checked the clock on my desk again. Angry red numbers announced the time: well after six p.m. Logically, I knew it was taking too long, but I reached into that place where I could hold on to things like hope and dreams. The place that gave me the opportunity to come up with alternatives. Other potential reasons for the delay.

They weren't very plausible. Still, I didn't let myself panic.

Setting my math aside, I paced along the center of our room. I walked the imaginary line. It was imaginary now, but when we were young, it was very real. One day I actually took masking tape, measured the dimensions of the room perfectly, and divided it. Her side. My side. Of course, the room wasn't perfectly square—a fact that never sat right with me. It was the settling of the house, and perhaps the subpar craftsmanship, that were to blame for the imperfections. So I had to adjust for the flaws.

I'd rolled the tape across our wood floor, up the walls, and even along the ceiling. Separated it into two equal parts. Even though things were never equal with Brit and me. There was never any symmetry with us because the scale forever tipped in her favor.

"Stare at your own ceiling," I'd tell Brit when she was lying on her bed daydreaming. Back when we fought all the time, I didn't even want her *looking* at anything of mine. It was my way of leveling the playing field. When I thought I still had a chance.

By the time we were sixteen, we didn't fight so much anymore. Mainly because I usually caved and let her have her way. Or let her *think* she was getting her way.

That was supposed to change tonight.

So why was it taking so long?

My answer came at the chiming of the phone. I picked it up on the first ring. "What's taking so long?"

"He's a total psycho," Brit said.

"What happened?" I asked, feeling a hint of worry that it wasn't done yet.

"Long story," she said. "But that little shit is following me."

"What?" I asked, trying not to overreact.

"I can see his truck behind me," she said, clearly rattled.

"Okay," I said as my brain worked to solve the problem. "Here's what I want you to do."

The Elements of a Crime:
#1 Mental State (aka: A Guilty Mind)

According to Wikipedia (though not my preferred resource, it's the most relatable), *mental state (mens rea)* refers to the mental elements of the defendant's criminal intent. This is an absolutely necessary element in crime. The criminal act must be purposeful. In other words, there must be a mental intention to commit the crime—*a guilty mind*. It's derived from the Latin *actus reus non facit reum nisi mens sit rea*. Translated, this means "the act is not guilty unless the mind is guilty."

So the guilty mind is probably the most common factor in determining liability. Did the accused intend to commit a crime?

In this case, the answer is yes and no.

Was there intent to hurt and do damage? *Yes.*

Was the intent for someone to die? My initial answer is *no*, but to be honest, I'm not sure. I guess I didn't think through that part. Or care.

So, Element #1, a guilty mind? Yes, I have one. Every time I see him, it wears on me. It takes me back to that night. I guess that's why I spend so much time on Hush.

With a click of the mouse, the chiming of the website

rings through my speakers and the screen on my laptop comes to life. *Welcome to Hush, an online community to anonymously share your secrets.*

I've been visiting the site for over a month—it's a place where freaks like me, who have nobody to talk to, can purge their sins. Everyone knows about it. Well, everyone aged fifteen to twenty. Nobody talks about it, though after some of the really bad admissions, it seems people are a little more cautious. The teachers and parents haven't caught on yet, or I'm sure they would shut it down. That's why it's vital that all communication be done on public computers. Trust me, you don't want to be linked to any of it.

My screen name: *Responsible.*

Telling, isn't it?

Today is a messy one on Hush. Some dark shit is being confessed out in cyberland. I scroll down the page and read the posts.

Guilty in Grand Rapids: I wish it was my dad who died of cancer instead of my mom.

Niceguy: Sometimes I think about hitting my girlfriend.

Unexpected Villain: I did a bad, bad thing.

I can't believe I now fit in with these assholes. Not that I can judge anymore. My sins are just as bad. Worse, actually.

Opening up an online note, I customize the font and color—because appearance is pretty important when you're out confessing to strangers—and then I begin to type.

Responsible: I let it happen…

5

JOHNNY

So I have a secret. A few of them, actually. Becca says I should go out and confess on Hush. Share my sins. Out with the bad and in with the good. She does have a point; it's a much safer avenue than, say, trusting a real-life person. Not that Bec necessarily believes in that kind of thing, but she'll occasionally spout out advice from her group therapy. It seems it might have been more helpful for her than she realizes.

This particular secret, however, is about my brain.

It is, well, seriously fucked. Doesn't work right. Never has. My brain is like a fat guy at an all-you-can-eat rib joint. Things are going along just fine, I consume, take things in just as I'm supposed to. But then, without warning, I reach out to grab something—a word, a phrase, a number—and it slips out of my greasy hands.

My poor, unreliable mind just doesn't grab on like it's supposed to. Completely refuses at times, the asshole. And it's not just for the stuff going *out* of my head, it's all the stuff coming *in* too.

I remember one time, I must've been about eight years old or so, we had to take a test after reading a little story called *The War with Grandpa*. Mom spent all this time with me on it. We read together, separate, aloud, in quiet. I didn't talk about it, but she knew I had trouble in school. After working for a few weeks, I knew the story inside and out. It was funny, about this kid who declares war on his grandfather after he moves into his bedroom. It was full of pranks, jokes, slapstick—everything an eight-year-old boy would find amusing.

By the time the teacher passed out the test, I was already thinking about the celebration Mom would have in honor of my first A. But when I read the questions, none of them made sense to me. I'd spent all this time on the book, and I couldn't answer one question on the test.

It was crushing.

I could feel the tears starting to pool, but then something stopped them. Anger, pride, I'm not sure—but I knew I couldn't cry in front of the class. So instead I tried to be funny. I wrote a different dirty word for each answer on the test, showing it later it to all my little buddies for shits and grins. They loved it.

Can't say the same for my teacher. Or Mom. But it was much easier to have her mad than disappointed.

From third to sixth grade it was a guessing game: *What's Wrong with Johnny?* Maybe he's just lazy, bored, hyper, immature, careless. He could have behavior issues, ADD, ADHD, dyslexia. We never really narrowed it down. All I know was it made things hard. Reading, remembering, listening, organization, you name it.

Mom used to write me lists all the time. She'd lay out my schedule for the day, like you'd lay out clothes for a pre-schooler. I needed it, because I couldn't remember. Without my lists, I was lost.

When I got older, I confided in my best (maybe only) friend, Paul. I tended not to let a lot of people in. Not that anyone really noticed. Did I have teammates? Yes. School pals? Sure. Friends? A select few.

Paul was my desperately needed ally. He was a good one. He'd even read things to me sometimes. And when Coach's words didn't quite register, he'd help explain. But then my issues became harder to hide. Reading aloud in class was a nightmare; getting called on in class was a nightmare. School in general? Nightmare.

I became the dumb kid.

The girls called me *Waste of a Pretty Face*.

To say I had anger issues over it … understatement.

Then I met Becca, and it all changed.

Oh, the anger was still there. I just had a new place to direct it.

On *Travis Kent*.

Stalking him became my new favorite pastime. I liked the anonymity of it all. In my head, I was working a case. I was the hero to Travis's villain. I took notes of every detail. What he ate, the times he went to bed and the hour he woke up, when he went to the bathroom, who he talked to.

We had gym together, and for that I was thankful. You can find out a lot about a person in the locker room, though

Travis didn't talk crap about girls or sports like most of the guys. He kept to himself. His gym clothes were always laundered, not like most of us who would go a few days before bringing in something new. They were always neatly folded when he pulled them out of his bag. Because I'd been watching him for months, staking out his house numerous times, I knew that he was basically on his own with his little brother—the thirteen-year-old carbon copy who followed him around everywhere. Mrs. Kent didn't live with them, and the mister worked long hours. So Travis was quite the homemaker.

In gym class, he was coordinated. I'd even go so far as to say he was talented in most sports. Yet he never went out for any team. He was scrappy and could hold his own. This was good to know. If threatened, he could put up a fight.

After class, he always took a shower. Always. When we didn't break a sweat in class, most of us would skip it. Not Travis. He was the ultimate neat freak.

His body was lean and surprisingly muscular, especially for somebody who lived off mochas and Monster. On his chest, he had a jagged scar about six inches long. Definitely not a surgical scar. When guys asked about it, Travis simply said, "You should've seen the other guy."

That gave me chills.

There were all kinds of rumors that followed Travis: he'd pummeled a teacher at his old school; he got rough with his girlfriends; he had hallucinations from all the drugs he took. Bottom line? He's an unstable psycho.

So I guess it wasn't strange that most people just let him be. They were afraid of him and nobody wanted to get too close.

Looking back, I wish I hadn't.

6

Brit wasn't afraid of him. She wasn't afraid of anything. That was part of her problem—she never knew when to quit. She would poke and prod until she got what she wanted. He was much the same way. This meeting was destined to be an all-out battle.

We ate a late dinner that night, grilled cheese and tomato soup, without her. During the middle of it, a cold throbbing pain sliced through my head. Quick and unwavering. The ache made my eyes cross and I spilled my milk all over the table, which put Mom in a tizzy. She didn't like anything to be out of order. We understood each other in that way.

I knew what the ache was, even if I wasn't ready to admit it. Brit was always talking about metaphysical phenomena with twins. She was constantly showing me studies and reading me all kinds of stories and bizarre anecdotes. I'd never been interested. Never believed. But the pain I felt now? I knew, without a doubt, that it was Brit's.

Figured. It was the first thought that came to me. Not

35

panic or sadness or concern. Just the irritation that she was trying to control me again.

Brit always wanted to share everything. Though it was imperative that she went first. First to talk, walk, and ride her bike. First to get her period and first kiss. But she wanted me to be close behind. I still have scars on my legs from my first bike-riding lesson to prove it. The day she put me on a bike and sent me sailing down our sloped driveway.

She was bothering me all day to try out my new bike. We'd gotten them for our birthdays. Mom found them at a garage sale and Dad painted them to look like pink twins. It'd been over a month and I hadn't so much as looked at the thing. Then the nudging and jabbing started and I knew Brit wasn't going to take no for an answer.

I gave up and joined her outside, where she had both bikes out on display. She flicked up the kickstand and leaned the frame toward me so I could climb on. She held on to the bike to steady me, because my feet only grazed the ground. I felt so unstable and it made me sick to my stomach.

"Don't worry," Brit said. "I've got you. I won't let go until you're ready."

"Not yet," I said, trying to warm up to the idea. "Not yet."

I put my feet on the pedals, closed my eyes, and took a deep breath. And that's when she let go. She not only let go but *pushed* me down the driveway. My eyes snapped open and everything was a blur. The trees that canopied the sidewalk; the patchy grass of our lawn; the cars parked in the street.

"You're doing it, Bee," Brit screamed. "You're really doing it."

She seemed almost proud of me for a moment. Though when I hit the curb that removed half the skin on my legs, *I* was the one who ruined everything.

Sadly, her later ideas about how to keep me locked in her shadow were even more painful.

As much as I wanted to ignore the feeling now, I couldn't. The pain told me that something had gone terribly wrong with the plan. And here I was, cursing Brit's name in my head while making small talk with Mom and Dad. Still, I couldn't say anything about it. Not yet. Maybe not ever.

After we cleared the table and did the dishes, Mom grabbed her laptop to get caught up on email while Dad and I watched the news. This wasn't my typical M.O. I didn't spend time hanging out with the family when I could help it, but I didn't want to be alone.

That's when the doorbell rang, and I immediately realized I'd been waiting for it.

Dad got up and pulled the curtain back to reveal police officers at the door.

"Oh, great," he said. A police visit wasn't all that uncommon in our neighborhood, so Dad wasn't too concerned when he answered the door. Two fairly young officers—one white and one black—stood there. I watched from the couch.

"Mr. Waters?" the white one asked as the cool autumn air filled the cozy room.

"Yes," Dad stuttered. Even if police at the door wasn't unusual, having them address you by name was.

"I'm afraid there's been an accident," the cop said.

The conversation moved quickly, and I could barely tell

who said what. I sifted through the officers' condolences and my parent's hysteria to gather the pertinent pieces of information I needed:

Brit.

Car accident.

Coma.

Bad shape.

Hospital.

We needed to leave immediately, but Mom and Dad were in shock or something. They fumbled around the house, running into each other, until I started barking orders. They were such children sometimes. I grabbed coats and keys and purses, stuffed my parents into the car, and rushed to Ford Hospital.

Turns out there was no need to hurry.

7

JOHNNY

A re you feeling all right?" Cassie asks, leaning over the front seat of the car on our way home from school. Her girlfriend, Ava, is driving. "You look like shit."

Becca calls my little sis *Black Sheep*. Today, she fits the part perfectly, with the newly dyed blue streaks in her dark hair and her snakebite piercings. A complete contrast from my clean-cut baseball player image.

Cassie isn't one for beating around the bush, and now that Mom isn't around, she feels it necessary to mother me. But she's right. I do look like shit. And I feel worse, probably because I haven't seen Becca since the beginning of the day.

Becca's become my touchstone. The one person I can count on. I feel lost without her.

She had a field trip to Dearborn after second period as part of her Accelerated Student math program. They're always heading to some college campus for lectures and what have you.

I don't know how she handles all the pressure. The

math she takes is never ending. The teachers are incredibly intense. The other students are painfully boring. Becca loves it, though—the independence, the extra work, the quiet. It's too bad the school insists she take half her classes with the commoners. It's those mainstream classes that are complete torture for the girl. We're such opposites.

"Hello, Johnny." Cassie raises her voice, thumping her hand on the back of the seat. "Are you in there?"

"Yeah, yeah, yeah," I mumble, finally answering her. "I'm feeling fine, but thanks for that lovely compliment."

She groans but I ignore it, closing my eyes for my daily ten-minute catnap as Ava, aka *Golden Retriever*, squeals around the corner. Ava is a menace on the road, and her rundown Ford Focus smells like hardboiled eggs and oranges. But I'm thankful Cassie has her. And that she carts my ass to and from school.

I used to ride home with Paul before Cass came out. Her announcement was just a month before the accident, and it took me completely by surprise. Looking back, there were so many signs, but I'd never looked at my sister in *that* way. I had no interest in her sex life; actually, I was happy she didn't have one. She was always just Cass and that worked for me.

She told all of us at dinner one night.

"Well, okay, angel," Mom said. "If that's how it is, that's how it is. I'm just happy you told us."

That was Mom. She took things in stride, which meant Dad did too. I fell in line as well. We were like these planets orbiting around Mom's axis—she was the invisible force that held us together.

Who didn't take it in stride? My friends, especially the guys on the team. They had their jokes and jabs about Cass and various girls. It wasn't long before I started to pull away from them, even from Paul. Dad knew what was going on. He said it was admirable I was siding with Cassie. What Dad didn't know was that the guys gave me grief about a lot of things—that's what happens when your brain doesn't work right and people think you're the school idiot. I wasn't noble; I didn't pull away only for her.

After the fallout with the guys, I stopped riding to school with Paul. So Dad was always watching for a junker to come into the shop—one that he could get for a song and fix up real nice for me. *We'll have you in wheels by senior year,* he said. Obviously that hasn't happened, which is fine by me. I'm a little nervous about driving, anyway. I know I'm supposed to be all machismo about these things, but I don't care.

When Ava isn't playing chauffeur to us, Becca is. She's fine with driving—especially since she's calculated the probability of both her and her sister being involved in fatal car wrecks. Evidently it's not an issue.

"I'm serious, Johnny." Cassie smacks me in the arm. "What's going on with you?"

"Are you really asking me this today?" I open one eye. "Do I have to teach *you* the rules of sensitivity too? Because, frankly, Becca's about all I can handle."

"This isn't just about the anniversary." She blows out a long breath. "It's been going on longer than that and you know it. And Becca's just as bad. That girl looks like the walking dead. Are you two okay?"

"You didn't dump her, did you, Johnny?" Ava interrupts. "Because you need to tread lightly with her."

"What?" I say. "No, I didn't dump her. And she didn't dump me either, not that you'd care."

I act hurt, but really I'm happy that Cassie and Ava have taken Becca in—though I have to admit, sometimes they get a little intense about it. They watch over her when I can't. She needs it. Before, she always had Brit to rely on. Her sister did everything for her—the talking, the social planning, even setting them up on dates together. Becca's never really learned how to do that for herself. So now, with Brit gone, she hasn't even thought about having a social life. And she doesn't realize that when she's feeling sad or anxious, she's actually lonely and in need of human interaction.

Yes, psychology. It's what I'm good at.

I really owe Cassie and Ava everything, but honestly, I can't deal with this shit today.

"Man, if I knew you two were on the attack, I would've taken the bus home," I snap at both of them. Then I close my eyes again.

"I'm just worried," Cassie says. Her voice cracks a little.

"I know," I whisper before falling asleep.

―――――――

At home, Dad is already sitting at the kitchen table with a bottle of Jack. He's aged about a decade since last year. It was exactly this time of day, exactly one year ago, when Mom left to pick up dinner and never came back.

It was a special dinner for me—we'd heard that week that three colleges were interested in me and they'd be out scouting in the spring. I heard the guys talking behind my back, saying I was a waste of a scholarship, that I could hardly make it through high school, so how could I handle college?

But Mom didn't question it for a second. She insisted on celebrating. That was her deal. *This calls for a celebration,* she said regularly. And celebrate we did. Cassie got an A in lit. Celebrate. I got my driver's license. Celebrate. Our furnace made it another winter. Celebrate.

"What's going on, Dad?" I ask as I make my way to the table. I pick up the bottle of Jack and raise an eyebrow. Dad's made it a full year without losing it, though there were times I thought he was close. If Cassie and I didn't still need him, I have no doubt he'd be a certified drunk by now.

"Don't start with me, Johnny," Dad slurs. "Everyone deserves a day without judgment."

I take a seat next to him and his eyes beg me to keep quiet. This time, I comply. He does deserve it.

"This is my day," Dad says quietly, more to himself than to me. "This is my day."

We sit there, like that, not saying a word. Dad's dirty nails strum on the table, and I'm sure Mom is rolling over in her grave at the sight. "Wash up," she'd say each night, laughing as Dad would paw at her, his hands grubby from working at the shop all day.

Now there's nobody to say that to him. And none of that special soap Mom used to buy—the kind that could take off a layer of skin if you rubbed hard enough. So here he sits with dirty hands and a bottle of booze.

"S'okay," I say, patting his arm. Then I take a swig out of the bottle. "You can have your day."

As long as I can have one too.

That's how it is now. Dad has the bottle. Cassie has Ava. And I have Becca.

I leave him there to drown in his booze and memories and go to my room to pack up my things for the night. I'm taking my day to remember Mom in my own way.

The equipment I need for tonight rests on my bed in a neat little row. Becca told me to think of our plan as a game. There are no criminals and victims; no captors or hostages. We are simply opponents; competitors in a contest seeking justice.

Strange—this does make it a little easier. I look over the rope, the Swiss army knife, the blanket, the track suit we bought from the Goodwill, cash, bottled water, first-aid kit, my gloves and disguise—checking each one off my mental list as I shove it into my backpack. The final item is waiting for me at the park, but first I have to stop at Poppy's.

I jump on my bike and head into the heart of Mexicantown. Poppy owns a little bodega there, and he's expecting me. He knew my uncle Christopher before he was sent away. Chris used to watch Cass and me on weekends when we were kids. We'd spend long lazy days at the park, hang at the bodega, and run Uncle Chris's many "errands." Mom and Dad didn't know about Chris's "weekend job" until he got caught.

Poppy has a name in the neighborhood, if you know

what I mean. "Influential" is a good word to describe his place on the food chain. He knows all and is known by all.

"Johnny," Chris said before he left, "you need anything, you call Poppy. He'll be there for you."

I weave through the crowd; lively music and the scent of spicy tamales fill the air. It's the last night of the *Día de los Muertos* festival—Day of the Dead—which runs every year from Halloween until the day after All Saints'. I ride through the crowds of people eating, drinking, and touring the *ofrendas* on display. The *ofrendas* are altars designed to honor the dead. Poppy wanted to put one out for Mom. Dad refused.

But thanks to me, Poppy will instead help avenge her killer—even if he doesn't know it.

There are tables and chairs in the parking lot in front of Poppy's store. He has someone working an enormous grill on one side of the lot and a beer tent for the occasion on the other. Poppy is mingling when he spies me. He nods and motions to the building. I lean my bike up against a brick ledge and walk into the bodega.

"*Qué onda, primo?*" Poppy asks me, leading me to the back room.

"I'm okay, Poppy," I tell him.

"It's hard to believe it's been a year."

"Yeah, it is."

We walk into Poppy's office and he immediately shuts the door. The click of the lock follows. He motions for me to take a seat. When I do, he opens his safe and takes out a wooden box.

All business.

"So," he says, opening the box. "You're sure this will take care of it?" He hands me the pile of twenties. Twenty-five of them.

"More than enough," I say, feeling the like world's biggest asshole. I told him Dad was hitting the bottle hard and missing work, and that we needed money. Though this may be true, I'm not going to use the money for a noble cause. I'm using it to buy a gun.

A few months ago, I asked Poppy outright if I could use one of his. I told him it was for protection. His answer was an angry *No hay manera en el infierno!* No way in hell!

Poppy has taken care of plenty for my family in the past. When one of the gangs was trying to recruit me, or when some thugs were giving Dad a hard time at the shop, Poppy was there. He takes care of his own, and we've become family to him.

This time, he's really left me no choice. I had to find a supplier on my own. Last week, everything came together and we set up the handoff. That's my next stop.

"Thank you so much. I'll pay you back."

"No need," Poppy says. "You know I'm loyal to Chris, and he told me to watch over you." He runs a hand through his short, thick cap of hair. "You're a good kid. You let me know if there's anything else I can do."

I nod, roll up the cash, and put it in my front pocket.

Once we're outside, Poppy hugs me. Then I jump on my bike and head to the park.

I meet a guy with my name and make the exchange

behind the swings near the trees. The other Johnny hands me a bag. I slip my hand inside and run my fingers along the Smith and Wesson .38 revolver. It's one of the most common guns out on the streets. Easy to use and, most importantly, hard to determine where it came from.

The other Johnny eyes me up and grins. "You sure you know how to use this?"

"Yeah, I'm sure." Uncle Chris made sure I knew how to shoot.

I just hope I don't have to. Becca and I agreed that it's just for looks. An incentive, if you will, to get Travis to do the right thing. *A damn good incentive.*

I hand Johnny the money and he gives me a handshake. It's that easy.

"Oh," I say, checking out the gun. I almost forgot the most important part. "Ammo?"

"That's extra, dude," he says.

"What do you mean, extra? You said you'd hook me up."

"With a piece, yeah," he agrees. "But ammo is extra. That shit is at a premium these days. How much do you want? I could get it to you tomorrow."

Tomorrow. Hopefully this will all be behind me tomorrow. This is so bad. Becca is going to lose it.

"Tomorrow is too late," I say. I want to say more, but I know better. Around here, survival is all about who you know and how to avoid pissing off the wrong people.

"If you change your mind, you know where to find me."

I nod and we part ways.

The gun was only supposed to be for show anyway. Now

we have no choice—but I'll keep that from Bec. No reason to get her all worked up.

Once I get home, I add the gun to the rest of the gear. The other items we'll use are already on site, so we're good to go. I text Becca and give her the thumbs-up.

Game on.

8

BECCA

When we arrived at the hospital, we were forced to play a ridiculous game of *Find the Missing Redhead.* We went to the ER first, which, in retrospect, didn't make the most sense. It had been a few hours since the crash. But after our police visit, nobody was thinking all that clearly.

To my parents, it was completely logical: *My daughter's been hurt. We need to get to her. Emergency. Emergency!*

My mother ran up to the desk centered in the middle of the waiting room. The front of it was still decorated in skeletons and ghosts from Halloween, something I found wildly inappropriate. Mom checked in with an overweight blonde woman who smelled like perspiration and rubbing alcohol. I held my breath during the entire exchange.

The place was chaotic. There'd been a massive pile-up on the interstate and the ER was full of bloody bodies, blue scrubs, and white coats flailing about. The woman at the desk was no help. She shuffled us along, past the fake skeletons and very real bloody limbs, suggesting we try the ICU.

49

In the ICU it was the same story. Nobody could locate Brit. And throughout the search for her, I simply became a prop.

"She looks like this," Mom said, pushing me toward anyone who would listen. Dad said nothing, just nodded his head vehemently at Mom's words. We listened, followed directions, and moved from place to place, losing hope with each step farther into the bowels of the hospital. I maintained a two-stride distance from my parents, secretly wondering if they'd look this grim if they were here to see me.

I came to the conclusion it was doubtful.

Twenty-two minutes passed before we arrived on the surgical floor and learned that Brit was, in fact, in the operating room. A nurse named Julie greeted us and got us situated in a special family lounge before she explained what was happening. Again the words came out hurried. It didn't sound promising.

Massive head trauma.

Internal injuries.

Swelling.

Critical condition.

Doing everything we can.

From what we pieced together after discussions with the police and the nurse, Brit had been heading west on Old Hwy 5 when she hit another car in a head-on collision. It was a high-speed, high-impact crash, and they'd had to use the Jaws of Life to get Brit out. The person Brit collided with was pronounced dead at the scene. A woman in her late thirties.

"I don't understand," Mom said, her mouth so full of

pain and grief it made her sound drunk. "Do you have any idea what she was doing there, Becca? I thought she went to Janie's house after school."

Yes, because that's what I told you.

"That's what she said," I confirmed.

Of course, she never went to Janie's. But I couldn't tell Mom about the old switcheroo.

We'd once tried switching places at home, a birthright all twins try at least once, but Mom was onto us immediately. It was because of the Brit/Mom connection. Even if I dressed and acted the part, there was something missing. Mom and I both knew that. With everyone else, however, it worked flawlessly.

Brit had me take tests for her when she needed to get her grades up, and sit in for her social engagements when she was double-booked. These moves were usually for her benefit … though there was the one time it was for me.

The kiss.

In sixth grade, Brit declared Josh Duvall her boyfriend. He was the most popular kid in school and Brit conquered him like a foreign land, sticking her flag in his chest and claiming him as her own. All the girls were crazy for this boy. He was *the* topic of conversation at the bus stop, lunchroom, and playground.

Josh was Brit's third boyfriend and I hadn't even had one yet. I also had no interest. I liked schoolwork and reading and spending time with my dad putting puzzles together. But by the end of the school year, Brit was tired of my childlike ways.

"It's time, Bee," she said one afternoon.

"Time for what?" I asked, scared of her glossy-eyed expression.

"Your first kiss."

"No, it's not," I said, wanting to run and hide. "I don't even have a boyfriend yet."

"But I do," she added, her plan already in motion.

Brit said she was doing this as a favor. Giving me the best possible first kiss with a guy I could never get on my own. I had to admit that her assessment of the situation was completely accurate and she made a very good argument. So, after getting over the initial embarrassment and anxiety about kissing my sister's boyfriend, I made an erratic decision to seize the day and agreed to her little ruse.

Carpe diem!

The next day after school, I met Josh at the park. I wore Brit's powder-blue hoodie instead of my usual brown cardigan. Even back then we dressed differently.

Josh took my hand. It was warm and a little sticky, but also nice. He talked about his big win in kickball during gym class and the gross fish sandwich they'd served for lunch. He made me laugh.

I didn't say much because I didn't want to give it away. I let him do most of the talking and he seemed to enjoy that, which I later realized was probably not how things usually went down when he was with Brit.

But I had to hand it to her; she knew how to pick 'em. I liked being there with Josh. I liked it quite a lot.

We sat on the swings for a while and had a contest to see who could get the highest. He won. Then, once we slowed down, he jumped off and came over to my swing. I could remember the butterflies in my stomach when he closed in on me like it was yesterday. That homey smell of fabric softener on his clothes. The warmth of his touch, which didn't make me shut down like it did with other people. This touch made my body buzz.

He slowed my swing to a stop and leaned in. His eyes slowly closed, but mine stayed open. I didn't want to miss a second of it. I was inexperienced, but I knew what was coming. He inched closer until his lips were on mine. They were a little chapped and dry. Still, I liked that roughness on my own mouth. Then, as easy as that, we were kissing.

It was sublime.

He tried using his tongue, which I didn't understand at the time, and I tried to follow along. To say the kiss was clumsy and sloppy would be generous.

It was in that moment that I experienced what it was really like to be my sister. And what I was missing. Not a comforting feeling to know you're being completely ripped off in life. No, it was much better before I knew. Before I got a taste of something better.

Brit had given me that taste, and instead of being grateful, I hated her for it.

Just like I hated her in that waiting room.

For the next three hours, Brit fought for her life in surgery. We sat in that room and tried to pretend none of this was happening. Julie brought us snacks and kept us updated, but time was almost at a standstill. Mom stared into space and drank her coffee. Dad pretended to watch TV. I paced.

After all, there was more than just Brit's life on the line in the O.R.

Welcome to Hush

The website chimes and it's beginning to feel like a comfort. My brain must get an endorphin rush when I come here to confess. The musical chiming probably triggers it.

So what to type today? I guess I've never really told the whole story—the actual event. Yes, I think it's time. But where to start?

When all else fails, I guess it makes the most sense to start at the beginning. So here goes.

Responsible:

It started because I couldn't get out of my own head.

I felt powerless, like I was drowning. I was losing my edge with everything and I couldn't take it anymore. I wanted things to be like they were. I wanted to be safe again. I wanted to take back control of my life. I also wanted someone to pay.

In situations like this, I've learned, it helps to

make a plan. So that's what I set out to do. One of my teachers even helped. She gave me a little trick to help reach my goals. The SMART method. Goals should be:

- *S: Specific (or Significant)*

- *M: Measurable (or Meaningful)*

- *A: Attainable (or Action-Oriented)*

- *R: Relevant (or Rewarding)*

- *T: Time-bound (or Trackable)*

Smart.

So I have the Detroit public school system to thank for that.

Of course, even after I set the goals, nothing went as planned. People got in the way and they got hurt, but that's how it all started.

9

....

JOHNNY

....

Becca picks me up at eight o'clock on the nuts. She had two hours to kill after dinner, and I know immediately what she's been doing. Her white Grand Prix sits in my driveway—immaculate. It's been Armor Alled inside and out. I can see my reflection in the hubcaps, and the lemony scent fills my nostrils as I fall into the bucket seat.

"Did you get it?" she asks without a hello.

I nod and reach back to grab it when a knock on the window stops me.

Cass.

Becca rolls down the window from her side, because she has the window locks turned on.

"What's up?" I ask Cassie.

"Just wanted to say hi to Becca." She leans in and smiles, but it's not her usual smile. It's weird, and so is she. "How's it going?"

"Good," Becca says.

"You sure?" Cass pushes. "I mean, today is terrible, obviously. But I'm here if you guys need me."

Now, most people would think that maybe Cass needs some comfort as well. But this is her way of digging in. She's in just as much pain as me over our mom, but I can never seem to give her the opportunity to talk about it. And she doesn't try.

I flush and strain for words. There are none. My sister's heart is in the right place, but this is just so awkward, it hurts.

"We just thought we'd mark the day quietly," Becca says, once again showing how oblivious she can be. "We're okay. Really."

I shuffle Cassie off, a sick sensation blooming in my chest, and we head out to mark what's left of the day quietly. Where does Bec come up with this shit?

"She knows something's up," Becca says once we start driving.

"No," I say. "She's just worried we're breaking up. She's just playing mom again."

"You need to keep her far away from this, Johnny. She can't find out."

"I know. It's fine, don't worry about it."

We drive a mile or so before Bec pulls to the side of the road so we can change. We slip into our disguises just like we discussed. I put on a skull cap and glasses and Becca's wearing a blonde wig and makeup. She looks ... well, hot. I can't take my eyes off her. And that's freaking demented considering what we're doing.

I wait a few minutes before I talk. Becca likes the quiet, especially when she's upset. And knowing her parents, and the fact it's the anniversary of Brit's death too, I'm sure her evening was rough. Though I have to admit, I didn't like her tone about Cass. It was almost threatening.

We sit there in silence until her body releases its rigid hold.

"How are your parents doing?" I ask once she seems more relaxed.

"They're more somber than usual—as to be expected," she answers.

She doesn't think to ask about my family. But I don't fault her for it. What she does think to do is usually better.

"Were they upset that you were leaving tonight?" I ask.

"Upset? No. Disappointed? Maybe. Though I did indulge them by joining in for a special dinner—all of Brit's favorites."

"You actually sat at the table with them?"

"Well, it is the anniversary," she says, turning on the blinker.

"And you ate it all? Even the peas?"

Peas were Brit's favorite, but Becca can't stand them. Her parents seem to forget that, so now Becca toughs it out. She can be surprisingly accommodating when she wants to be.

"I had to." She rolls her tongue around in her mouth, like she's still trying to get rid of the taste. "And with the right amount of milk they go down like ibuprofen."

"Nice."

Becca drives, keeping to the speed limit perfectly. "So where's the gun?" she asks.

"Waistband," I reply.

She removes one hand from the wheel and snakes it along my belt before landing on the weapon that rests on my lower back. She takes her focus off the road and blinks in my direction. Just for a second, her eyes dance with excitement.

My heart swells with pride. It was my idea to get a gun—a back-up to give us more leverage. Becca was thrilled I came up with it. "That's smart, Johnny," she said. "So smart."

What would she say if she knew I had no bullets to go inside my smart gun?

In exactly seven and a half minutes, we're behind the mini-mall. Just like Becca planned. It's the strip that houses the high-tech arcade called "For the Love of the Game."

They're the host of tonight's gaming tournament. The finals start in about twenty minutes, and Travis should be in it—statistically speaking. I recorded all of his recent scores on *Zombie Nation* and Becca figured out the probability of Travis Kent making it to the finals. It was pretty damn good.

Becca takes her phone out to monitor the tournament; @GameJoy is live-tweeting the event.

"Just a few minutes left in this round," Becca reports to me like she's a sports announcer. "@InsomniacGames (aka Travis Kent), @RockstarGamer, @Xplaya, and @NaughtyDog are in the lead."

She continues with the play-by-play and I roll my eyes. Until we get the news we're waiting for.

Travis is one of the finalists. Becca's not surprised. The girl should get into gambling; she could make a killing with her statistics and prediction capabilities.

The tournament schedule calls for a fifteen-minute break between rounds, so now we need to hang tight until it's over. We sit in the car with everything turned off, our eyes on the building. I reach out and grab Becca's hands to warm them in mine. She smiles and leans over the console to rest her head on my shoulder. Then she slides her hand inside her jacket.

"Here." She hands me a black-cushioned folder that looks like a diploma or something.

I pull back and arch an eyebrow. "What's this?"

"A memento for the anniversary," she says, not meeting my eyes.

I open the folder. On one side is a photo—a night sky filled with stars. One cluster, in particular, is outlined in a white square. On the other side is a certificate...with my mother's name on it.

"She has a star now," Becca says simply.

"What do you mean?" I study the certificate.

"I had a star named after her. Of course, you can't really name a star, but this is as close as you can get."

"You bought my mom a star?"

"I did."

I swallow the tears threatening to fall. It's not that I'm uncomfortable crying in front of Becca—I've cried in front of her before, a few times. When you go through deep shit at a young age, you either let it out or bottle it up. I choose to let it out. But tears of joy, or appreciation, or happiness? Well, for Becca, those don't compute. So *those* are the tears I hold in.

"Did you know that the most massive stars are the shortest-lived?" she asks.

"No." My voice wavers. "I don't think I did."

"It's true. I chose the largest one I could find for your mom. It seemed appropriate—a short life, but a big life."

She leans up toward the dash, looking outside. "Let me show you," she says, not taking her eyes off the sky. "I should be able to see the closest constellation to give you an idea of where the star is located."

I follow, leaning forward in my seat. I slow my breath so I don't start bawling. But man, sometimes she brings me to my knees.

"That's the general area." She points. "Near the Ursa Major constellation. Right in there. That's where you'll find Anna's Star."

Anna's Star.

I clear my throat.

"It's the easiest constellation to spot. I thought it'd be good for you to be able to see it a lot—and have it close."

Have Mom close. I like that.

"It's beautiful, Becca." I reach out and pull her into my lap. "And so are you."

She comes over easily and straddles my legs. It's so not the right time to be doing this; I need to keep my head in the game. Yet I can't help it. She's like the most addictive drug—the more I have, the more I want. Maybe she's right, maybe it's all just a chemical reaction. It feels like so much more, though. With Becca, I feel alive.

I slide my hands under her shirt and feel the delicate muscles in her back tighten as she squirms from side to side on top of me. Then I pull her in and kiss her with everything I feel in the moment. I trail my tongue along the seam of her lips, my way of asking permission. She grants it and opens, allowing me to kiss her long, hard, and deep. I kiss her because despite her cold edge, she's thoughtful and sweet and kind and loving.

And mine.

It's hard not to get lost in her when we're this close, but we have a job to do, so I slowly pull back and she slides off my lap. We just need to get through the next sixteen hours—that's the average length of time it takes someone to confess. Obviously, we went into this plan with a whole shitpot of research. Once we get the confession, Becca will finally have closure. Hell, I'll have closure, and justice will be done.

I keep my eyes on Travis's car—a rusted-out Jeep. It's about twenty feet in front of us. Becca keeps her eyes on the live-gaming tweets.

"Okay, they're starting now," she says, pulling on her gloves. "Let's do it."

We open our car doors and quietly shut them without allowing them to close all the way. I reach my gloved hand for hers and squeeze it. But really, I'm the one who needs the encouragement. The connection.

Reaching into the grill of Travis's Jeep, just above the front bumper, I find the latch and release the hood so we can do the dirty work. I open it and take the socket wrench out of my bag while Becca holds a flashlight.

I move it to my destination: the negative connector to the battery. But as I get ready to loosen the nut, there's a huge crash on the side of the building.

Becca clicks off the light and I jump.

She immediately ducks down by the side of the Jeep and brings me down with her, but the goddamn hood is still open.

It's quiet. Too quiet.

Then a metallic rattling rings across the lot.

And then quiet again.

Shit, someone's out here. We're not ready; we're going to get caught. My hands are hot and clammy inside my gloves and I feel like there's not enough oxygen going to my brain. I sway in my crouched position.

Becca puts her hand on my thigh, trying to calm me down. There's a soft thumping sound in the distance. And soon, a lighter pattering noise. It closes in on us and I hold my breath. Until I hear a whiny meow.

Jesus Christ. Just a fucking cat out by the garbage.

Becca pops back up. "It was only a cat. Come on, let's finish this."

I pull out the wrench, and once her light is shining on the battery connector, I try again. It doesn't work, my hand is shaking too bad and I'm fumbling all over the damn place.

"Here." Becca holds out her hand. "Let me."

"Just give me a minute," I say, feeling like a tool. I can't let her take on everything all the time. I'm starting to lose what little sense of male pride I have left.

"Let me handle it," she says. Just like she did the first time I met her.

10

BECCA

We waited in the special room for five hours, with Nurse Julie checking in every now and then. Dad continued to watch TV and Mom stood at the window drinking coffee. She had the pot gone in the first sixty minutes. I made her another pot and then drank juice boxes and played solitaire on my phone.

My head raced and I went over every possible scenario of what could've gone wrong. Or was it just an accident? Possible; not likely. I thought about phoning him, but decided against it. It was too risky.

Mom and Dad released frequent sighs and odd moans, but otherwise, it was silent. We were scared to talk, to move. It was becoming unbearable, trapped in this small room with my parents.

Just when we thought we couldn't last another minute, Julie came in with the news that Brit was out of surgery. She lead us to her room; my family practically tiptoeing the entire way. We moved slow, cautious, none of us really wanting to see what was going to happen next.

In a small, white, and far-too-bright room, my sister was on the hospital bed propped on a pillow, tubes taking over the upper half of her body. It was difficult to comprehend. Brit's head was bandaged, and from the looks of it, most of her hair had been shaved off. Her head was tiny wrapped up that way, like the end of a Q-tip.

We moved around her bed and just stared. Tears fell from my parent's eyes, dotting Brit's sheet in wet, misshapen spots. My sister—my vibrant, loud, crazy sister—was so quiet. So still. The scents of antiseptic and death filled the air, and I just wanted to leave.

The surgeon told us the surgery went as well as could be expected, but there were no guarantees. Her injuries were severe and we wouldn't know how badly her brain was damaged until the swelling went down and she woke up. If she woke up.

That's when I started saying my goodbyes.

I had to say them each day over the next month.

Despite what my parents wanted to believe, Brit was gone. She wasn't coming back to us. And all I could think was someone had to take the blame.

Travis Kent.

Gamer geek Travis Kent.

Brutally intense Travis Kent.

Possessive and dangerous Travis Kent.

My secret boyfriend Travis Kent.

Sister-hater Travis Kent.

I met Travis at the end-of-year Skip Day. I never went to these things, but Brit needed a ride home and I'd already taken all my finals so my schedule was pretty open. Plus, my summer tutoring gig was a few weeks out and frankly, I had nothing better to do.

That year, Skip Day was at a park. People were playing Frisbee, lying out in the sun, dancing, and getting high. Typical. Brit had decided to do the latter. Usually she stuck to alcohol, so I'm not sure why she had the sudden urge. I also didn't really care.

The smell of pot gave me headaches and stoned people made me irritable, so I declined to go along with it. Trouble was, not a soul from my ASP group was in attendance—nobody I even knew casually. I was on my own.

I grabbed a book from my summer reading list, aka *ten books every college freshman should read*. I'd have mine read before junior year even started. I found a comfortable spot under a tree, opened Wallace's *Consider the Lobster*, and began to read the collections of essays that would supposedly help me become a more accomplished critical thinker.

I hadn't finished the first page before Travis showed up. He was always quick to make a move. Though I had no idea why he'd chosen me that day.

Travis Kent was hard to explain. He was a geek, a gamer, and a bad boy all rolled in one. He had a few friends, but mostly kept to himself. I knew his name because we'd had a class together the year before. I'd watched him even then.

Most girls did. While he was still considered a bottom-feeder, he made good eye candy. He always looked nice. He wore the standard dark jeans and T-shirts—except his were pressed, with no holes and rips. Built of lean muscle, he seemed taller than he was. He had what Dad would call a *presence*. He wore his hair long and secured it in a low tail, showing off his deep blue eyes. Yet, with all of that, he still couldn't climb the social ladder. He was like one of those creatures in the wild that keep the animals at bay with a built-in defense mechanism. I never found out why that was.

"Are you actually reading on Skip Day?" he said, taking a seat next to me.

"It would appear so." I answered his stupid question without looking up from my book.

"Isn't that defeating the purpose of this event?"

"Not sure that I care. I'm only here to give my sister a ride, anyway."

He was either bored or looking for someone to bother, and I was not going to be his afternoon entertainment, so I continued to ignore him as he chattered on.

"And you're not interested in partaking in the festivities over there?" he asked, motioning to my sister and her friends surrounded by a plume of smoke.

"Not my thing." I finally looked over at him, and when I did, I no longer seemed to mind the interruption.

"Hmm." He scratched his invisible chin-stubble. "What *is* your thing?"

That's when I got it. He was into me. Maybe. Possibly. It was the very first time a boy had taken interest in me without the promise of Brit Waters's attention. It felt…unreal. Nice. Wonderful. Which is precisely why I shouldn't have trusted it.

Still, I allowed it to go on. I let him flirt, and sit under my tree, and feed me treats from his not-so-picnic picnic basket. I let him in.

Thankfully, he left before Brit came back all pie-eyed—though not before making plans for the next day. Those plans lasted most of the summer.

Though he was the one to approach me, Travis was just as secretive about our relationship as I was. It made me feel safe. Special. Plus, I was thrilled to have something that was mine and mine alone. Travis's little brother would occasionally see me come and go, but we were never introduced. I never met his dad; we never went out with his friends; and we never talked in school.

It was our secret.

11

It's morbid, but I used to hang out at the accident site all the time. It's a fairly normal part of the grieving process for some people, I guess. That's what I read anyway.

Cassie came with me the first time. But after that, she said it was unhealthy. "There's a fine line between grieving and obsession, Johnny," she said. "So don't go freaking out on me."

After that little lecture, I didn't tell her that I continued to make frequent visits. It was an easy bus ride from our house. And I only had to make one transfer, so it was cheap enough to come out whenever I felt the need.

Still, the location was somewhat remote for being so close to downtown. Our favorite pizza place wasn't in this area, so Mom must have driven out of the way. She must've taken this route to avoid traffic—all to please her inconsiderate son. I never even gave it a second thought. Never really appreciated what she did for me. Every damn day.

On the side of the street where it happened, there were dead flowers, dirty ribbons, and a deflated silvery balloon. I think some of Cassie's friends put up this makeshift memorial. The road winds down from the top of a hill, and kids love to race down it after weekend parties. It's amazing there aren't more mini-tombstones in the area. Flanked with dead trees on one side and an abandoned office building and parking lot on the other, it's a place that looks like death.

That particular day, I sat on the cold ground staring at the street—trying to piece together the accident. Soon it'd be covered in snow and everything would look different, so I soaked it all in.

I looked down the road and imagined Mom driving up the hill. It was just approaching dusk—dim, but still light enough to see. Brit Waters was coming down the hill. Neither of them speeding. Or on the phone. Or texting. According to the report, anyway.

Still, they hit each other. Head on.

At fifty miles per hour, it was enough to kill them both. They said Mom died *instantly*. That's the only thing that got me through it, I think. They only thing that's held me together. Knowing she didn't suffer.

But why did they hit each other? What was it that made them overcorrect and sail across the middle line? That's something the investigators couldn't explain. They said, *there are some pieces of that night that we'll never know.*

Contemplating all of it, I didn't hear her approach.

At first, I thought she was a ghost. Brit coming to talk to me from beyond the grave with a message from my mom or some shit. I was in rough shape back then.

"What are you doing here?" she asked me.

"What are *you* doing here?" I repeated, getting slightly spooked at that point.

Once she came farther into view, it hit me. Brit's twin—Becca Waters. She was pale and skinny, holding a coffee cup in her long fingers.

I didn't really know either one of the Waters twins. I knew who they were, of course; they were the fantasy of most of the baseball team. Hot twins. It doesn't get much better than that. But I don't think I'd ever said a word to Brit. Definitely not to Becca—she was the shy one, and somewhat of a loner. Seeing her at the site, though, made me want to get to know her.

"I'm sorry for your loss," I told her after some brief small talk.

"Thank you," she answered.

I hoped we could somehow commiserate together, thought it would be nice to talk to someone about the accident for a change. Dad and Cassie couldn't talk about it. Or wouldn't. They were going through the motions—they'd grieved the appropriate amount of time and were starting to get their lives back on track, just as they were supposed to. Textbook, really. But I knew it would only take a few words from me—questioning the accident, talking about my nightmares, bringing up Mom—to cause them to fall, desperate, back into the hole of despair.

So I tried to talk about the crash with Becca, but had no luck. At first, anyway.

All she did was pull out her tape measure and notebook and start measuring things and writing down various numbers and graphs. She got low and stared at the road from every possible angle.

I watched, curious. "What are you doing?" I asked.

"Investigating," she said without looking up.

"The accident?"

"Yes," she said, scratching in her notebook.

"Why?"

"Because I don't think it was an accident."

She then talked about the impact of the crash, the way the cars were mangled, the injuries, the fuck all of it. My stomach dropped right out from me. And my lunch came up with such force, it not only splattered on my hands when I leaned over to relieve myself but made its way out my nose as well.

None of it fazed Becca.

She just grabbed some tissues from her bag and handed them to me.

"What? It hasn't crossed your mind?" she asked.

I shrugged, pushing a finger to each nostril to blow out any leftover chunks of vomit stuck in my nasal passage—almost gagging again as the putrid taste of puke went back down my throat. I could still taste it in the back of my mouth.

"Don't you think the circumstances surrounding the accident are odd?" she continued.

"What do you mean by odd?" I asked, not wanting to give away my theories.

"Suspect?"

"What are you saying?" I said, getting irritated that she wouldn't spit it out.

"I'm saying it wasn't an accident, as I mentioned when you first started grilling me." She went back to her measurements.

"And what, exactly, could your genius mind tell you that the investigators missed?"

"Quite a lot, actually," she said.

Of course I wanted to know. I wanted to know it all. "Well, then. Do you need some help?"

"Just let me handle it," she said, continuing to take measurements. "I'll let you know when I have enough evidence to prove it."

It seemed Becca had her own theories, and she was here looking for proof.

12

The suffocating guilt grabbed me by the throat and continued to squeeze during all those long days at the hospital ... waiting. That waiting can mess with a person's mind. We were waiting for her to die. Waiting so *we* didn't have to make the decision to let her go. And in classic Brit fashion, she made a difficult situation even harder to bear. It was the way she worked. Though, if I'm being truthful, *I* actually made the decision that sealed her fate—when I took my boyfriend's side against hers.

Despite how secretive we'd been, Brit was onto my transgressions with Travis from the very beginning. But she waited until the fall, when it became serious, before she stepped in with her authoritative approach.

"Listen to me, Bee," she said, after admitting she knew we were together. "You're out of his league."

"You mean, *you're* out of his league and it'll make you look bad if anyone finds out I'm dating him," I countered.

"That's not it." She began working me over. "He's odd, and a total loner."

"Yeah? Well, so am I."

"Not true. You deserve so much better."

"Try again," I said.

"People talk about him, you know. I heard that he used to beat up his old girlfriend." She paused, waiting for my reaction.

She didn't get one because I already knew this. Though by now I was getting to the real reason why our relationship bothered her so much. She didn't want to be linked any of that "talk." *I mean, how tragic.*

"That was one incident," I said, making light of it even though the mounting accusations against him were disturbing. Still, I wasn't going to let her get her way this time. "He also explained the whole thing to me. It was a misunderstanding. Charges were never filed."

Call me sick, but I liked Travis's dark side and the cloud of mystery and danger that hung over him. Brit didn't understand this because she always got attention. For me, it was new and exciting the way he fussed over me. I liked his possessiveness. It made me feel precious or something. That is, until I felt like a precious possession.

I knew our relationship was becoming more intense. I knew Travis was unpredictable. I knew I shouldn't have let Brit go over there to threaten him. But I tried, didn't I?

"You need to end it," she said, once again governing my life as she had been since she'd learned to talk.

I wanted to ask my sister if she could actually hear herself speak. Hear how demeaning and patronizing she was. But I didn't. Because I was scared. I mean, the girl had even tried to snuff me out in the womb. Like with dogs in a pack, the runt often dies. I'd been very close to dying. My sister, conversely, was Darwin's finest example. And since her actions toward me before birth didn't work, she eliminated me in other ways. Silenced me every chance she got. She was the girl who had an innate sense of survival, no matter the cost—even to me.

Still, I couldn't fault her for it.

Genetics, I suppose.

Mathematically, I knew all about genetics. Dominant and recessive genes; DNA; patterns. Emotionally, I'd never understand it. The desire to protect someone just because they shared the same genes, and all the feelings that went along with that.

How could you completely love and hate someone at the same time?

Brit didn't back down on Travis. She went on about his alleged sketchy history and said that if I didn't call it off, she'd tell our parents about all the rumors surrounding him. That's when I knew I didn't stand a chance. Brit had this way of appearing she knew what was best for me. "I'll look out for her," she'd always say. And our parents would go along with whatever she said.

So instead of fighting, I played her game for a few months, agreeing not to see him if she promised not to tell Mom and Dad.

Of course, that wasn't going to work for me, so Travis and I upped our security protocol, throwing Brit (and her spy friends) off our scent. We had this whole adventure going on, stealing moments to meet whenever we could, devising excuses, and finding new hideouts. As the stakes grew higher, so did my feelings for Travis. For the first time in my life, I was impulsive and illogical. It was an amazing high—not that I would know about that. My brain cells have always been too important to me. Like the waifs in school who wouldn't risk eating a piece of pizza for the sake of their waistlines, my brain was something I'd never take for granted.

Though, and I hate to confess it, maybe I wouldn't have stuck with Travis as long as I did without all the excitement— without that triumphant feeling of defying Brit (which was incredible, by the way). It was freeing. I wasn't a *we* anymore when I was with Travis; I was *me*.

It was wonderful in the months it lasted.

In October, Brit finally found out we were sneaking around behind her back. She was so angry I'd lied to her, she tried to call Dad on the spot. Thankfully, I was able to intercept. Didn't matter, though. I knew she'd tell them eventually.

I needed a more permanent plan, so I lured her in.

"I will break up with him, Brit," I said. "Promise."

"Too late for promises. I don't trust you anymore."

"Well, what am I supposed to do then? Bring you with me when I drop the news on him? I think that would be a little extreme, don't you?"

"Nothing is too harsh for that asshole," she said.

"I wish you could do it for me."

"What?" she asked, her ears almost visible perking up. "Break up with him?"

I nodded.

"Hey, now, that could work." She twirled her hair, the way she always did when she was thinking really hard. "Then I could be sure. I could do it the right way and leave no room for negotiation."

"What're you talking about?" I asked. She couldn't be serious.

"*I'll* break up with him." Brit pulled her shoulders back. "I'll go over there and pretend I'm you."

"He'll know."

"Not a chance," she said. "It's the perfect plan. Who's the genius now?"

Well, apparently neither one of us was pushing three figures on our IQ scores, because I called Travis and told him about the plan. I couldn't stand the thought of her blindsiding him.

As if *that* wasn't bad enough, I fueled his rant and agreed that my sister was a bitch for not understanding him. And when I said I was tired of her pushing me around and keeping us apart, and that we had to do something about it? Well, I just made the situation so much worse.

His wheels were turning, and I knew these weren't happy thoughts. Still, I didn't stop it. And I let him handle it his own way.

I thought he'd just scare Brit—threaten her or something. Travis had a way of making people do what he wanted. He was even better than my sister. I figured he'd threaten her, she'd cave in, and then I'd be free from her clutches.

He did more than that. He went ahead and went through with it, making her pay like he'd been saying he would.

Brit called me when she saw him following her. Her voice wasn't right. It was high and unsteady. She gave me the play-by-play as it was happening. I wanted to get off the phone with her and confront Travis, but it sounded as if he was too far gone.

I was beginning to believe that Brit could be right about him. She was right about a lot of things.

At first, he just kissed her bumper a few times. I told her to stay below the speed limit and keep a firm grip on the steering wheel. Until he tried to push her onto the shoulder, at which point I tried to help her lose him. I knew the area well and felt that a few well-timed turns could easily do the trick.

It worked. She made a turn and he was long gone. At least that's what we thought.

The Elements of a Crime:
Definition of Homicide

In addition to understanding the elements of a crime, it's also important to understand the definition of said crime. In my case, we're talking about the death of a person, or persons.

Homicide.

It's important to note that not all homicides are considered crimes. Technically, homicide includes all types of killings of human beings. Criminal homicides include first and second degree murder, with varying degrees depending on the magnitude of the crime. This is where premeditation and intent come into play.

Manslaughter usually refers to a killing that falls short of murder. The lowest form of manslaughter is involuntary manslaughter. This means that though the accused didn't intend to kill, they are responsible for a death because their actions were negligent or reckless.

Now there are some laws that allow for exceptions in some killings—considered "justified" homicide. Self-defense is one example. And that is key…

It could make all the difference.

13

....

BECCA

....

On December 3, 2012, we took Brit off life support. She'd been in a vegetative state for more than a month. We should've done it weeks before, but Mom and Dad couldn't do it. They were praying for a miracle—my non-believing parents.

It's true; there really are no atheists in foxholes.

We all stood around my sister. Mom and Dad each held a hand. I couldn't look them in the eyes. The ceremony of it was incredibly stupid. Brit had left us thirty-two days before. All the life had already seeped out and now she was nothing but a pile of meat—pale and soft.

Anyone who'd met Brit knew there was never anything pale or soft about her. She was always flushed, her eyes constantly dancing with mischief. And tough. She even loved hard.

So dying like this ... it wasn't right.

Yet I stood there too, not ready for the end.

The room was cold and static. The only sounds came from the whoosh of the ventilator and the beeping of the heart monitor. It wasn't comforting or peaceful. It was creepy and strange and Brit would've hated it.

The nurse came in and disconnected the ventilator and we all held our breaths.

"No," I called out in a voice that didn't sound like my own. Mom looked up at me, tears streaming down her face.

"This isn't how it was supposed to be," I whispered in my sister's ear. "This wasn't supposed to happen."

But it was happening. The mechanical breathing sound faded away and the beeps of the heart monitor slowed. Brit was still. Her little mouth didn't even try for a last breath. It took only a few minutes to her limp body to shut down.

That's when it really sunk in. It was my fault and I couldn't take it back. I worried that maybe I really did intend for this to happen. Maybe somewhere deep down, I wanted my own life and this was the only way to get it. Maybe I wanted my sister dead. The thought made it hard to breathe. So I pushed all those feelings away and settled on anger instead.

I stayed there like that—bent over Brit's bed with my cheek pressed up against hers. I stayed there until they pulled me away.

The damage was done. It was over. I really believed it was, anyway. Sadly, I had no idea how bad the pain would get.

14

Becca takes the wrench from my hand and goes to work on the Jeep. After taking too long, she discovers she can't disconnect Travis's battery cable either. It's corroded with rust and crap and won't budge.

I keep a lookout for any random people in the parking lot. We've been lucky so far. Except for the cat, we've been alone. It won't stay that way, so we have to work fast. Every second counts at this point.

Becca glances down at her cell phone and bites the side of her cheek. Her fingers fly across the phone. "It's time."

The plan was to have Becca text Travis after the tournament. He has a hard-on for some gamer chick, so Becca hacked into the girl's account and now she can both monitor and send messages from GamerGirl's line. She thought it'd be the best way to get Travis where we need him to be.

I rush over to Becca's car and riffle through her bag while she lowers the hood of Travis's Jeep. She moves toward me—purposeful, quiet, and determined. I hand her the syringe and she nods.

But she's not where she's supposed to be. I'm not where I'm supposed to be. We were supposed to have more time. Recognizing my panicked look, she smiles, easing her hands down to tell me it's going to be okay. Then a finger to her lips.

Shhhhh.

He's coming.

I slide into the driver's seat just in case we need to make a quick getaway. That's if I can make myself hit the gas. Not like I have a choice—if the options are getting caught or fighting a panic attack, I'll take the panic attack any day.

A figure appears from the side of the building. I'd recognize that gait anywhere; everything about Travis is burned into my brain. Sometimes I think I know him better than I know myself.

"Ow, ow," Becca starts howling from the front area of the Jeep. Travis turns toward her. I wait and watch, ready to act if I need to.

For a complete sociopath, Travis moves really quickly.

Becca is crouched down, like a tiger, ready to pounce.

He moves closer.

"Are you okay?" I can hear his muffled voice through the crack in the car door.

She moans some more. Then, when he gets close enough, she stabs him with the syringe. Direct hit, right into the neck. Becca stole the drugs from the hospital two weeks ago.

Travis bats at her, confused, but she quickly jumps out of his reach. He pushes himself upright and points at her before placing his hand to his neck. He rubs the injection site and leans his head against the brick wall.

"What happened?" His voice trails off and he slides down the wall, taking some skin off his face as he goes down.

Becca wasn't kidding. The shit works fast.

He slumps into a pile and Becca rummages through his pockets, placing the contents into her bag.

"Okay," she calls out to me.

My body on autopilot, I join Becca and pick up the pile of Travis. I don't know if it's the adrenaline or what, but he's much lighter than I expected.

I follow Becca to her car. She opens the door to the backseat, which is covered in plastic. It reminds me of a scene from *Dexter* and I work to keep the bile at bay as it climbs up the back of my throat. Dropping Travis across the seat, I finally see his comatose face.

No.

I squeeze my eyes shut and reopen them again, trying to make sense of what they're telling me.

It can't be.

My gaze focuses in on the thin lips, long nose, pudgy face. It's him, but it's not.

"Just get in," Becca snaps. "We're running out of time."

"But..." I say, taking another look.

"Now, Johnny." She spits out the words.

Stunned, I go to the passenger side of her car and get it. Becca slowly pulls away, careful not to bring attention to us.

I close my eyes and try to pull it together.

Then, I look in the backseat again. This time, I'm sure. I'm positive. The guy sprawled across the plastic sheet in the back is definitely not Travis.

15

I left the room first. I couldn't stand to be in there any longer. The florescent lights; the stale ammonia scent; the look on my parents' faces.

Down the hall and around the corner, the special waiting room was empty and the refrigerator was full of juice boxes. They'd become a comfort for me in here—something sweet to coat all the bitterness rotting my insides.

I closed my eyes and tried to block out everything. I tried to forget, until light footsteps caught my attention. I kept my eyes closed because I didn't want anyone to bother me.

Please, please just go away.

"Becca?" a small soft voice called out. It was a voice in between—deep and crackling, yet still high enough to sound feminine.

Ethan Kent.

He walked over to me carrying a bouquet of daisies. It was like a scene out of a Disney movie: a just-pubescent boy with short sandy hair and proper manners making a kind gesture to set everything right.

"I brought these for your sister," he said.

He handed the flowers to me; I didn't take them. They were bundled together in that cheap plastic wrap, devoid of all smell. They reminded me of Travis. Appealing on the outside, but nothing of value on the inside.

"I'll just set them here," he said, putting them on the seat next to mine.

"Is this some kind of joke?" I asked him. "Did your perverse brother put you up to this?"

Ethan didn't need to answer. I knew Travis had sent him here to show me he was in control, that he could do whatever he wanted. But this time, he'd messed with the wrong person. I'd been under my sister's thumb for as long as I could remember, and I wasn't about to be controlled again. Never again.

That day, a fire ignited in me. Heat that had been there under the surface, waiting. This move by Travis was the match that set it ablaze.

"What do you mean?" he asked, taking a step backward.

"She's dead. She's *dead!*" I jabbed his chest with my finger.

"I'm sorry," he said. "We didn't know. Travis didn't think you'd see him, so he sent me. He's worried about you."

"He should be worried about me." I stood up, physically unable to be still. "He should be very worried."

Ethan's face twisted into something less Disney and more Stephen King. He trembled as his eyes cast down.

"Don't say that," he said.

I smiled. Ethan was scared of me. I stood a little taller, taking up more space in the room.

He took another step back.

I put on this new role like a welcome down jacket in a frigid Detroit winter. It was warmth and safety. I was finally the person on the offense rather than defense. I was in control and it was a heady feeling. One I'd eventually become hooked on.

"Don't ever come back here," I said with my hands clamped around Ethan's shoulders, giving him a stern shake. "You tell your brother the same thing."

I shook him again. Hard.

"Stop," he said. "Stop, Becca."

The words didn't register. They didn't make sense to me. I'm not sure how long we stayed like that. I'm not sure how bad I hurt the kid. Nothing made sense until I woke up in a ball on fourth floor, in a place affectionately referred to as the Nut Hut.

I'd been there before.

16

JOHNNY

My girlfriend has lost her mind. Seriously lost it.

"What the hell, Becca?" I'm yelling now as she drives toward the site, just as we planned. All except for the fact that we, oh, have the wrong person in the backseat of our little crime scene.

She turns on the radio, and the streetlights shine on her smooth, pale skin. She could just as easily be driving to the library. Instead, we're carting around a hostage. The White Stripes sing in the background—it's that song "We're Going to Be Friends." The sweet track about school and numbers and letters and walking with a friend. The polar opposite of what's happening in our car. It's sinister. Sick, really.

"*This is not Travis*," I hiss at her.

"Yes, Johnny. I realize that," she says without any sliver of emotion.

"Then why are we driving?" I'm completely confused about this change of events, but it doesn't seem to bother her in the least. Something's not right.

"I actually had this planned," she explains.

As the words sink in, I fall back in my seat. It's like she's coldcocked me in the face. "What? You had it *planned* to grab Travis's kid brother?"

I should have recognized Ethan immediately—I've gotten to know him too, this past year. During all that time watching Travis, his brother was always around, and I know Ethan's habits almost as well as I know Travis's. But with the same walk and mannerisms as his brother, he had me fooled for a minute.

"Yes, I planned it," Becca tells me as she turns down the radio.

Un-fucking-believable.

"He's only a kid, Becca. He's, like, thirteen or some shit."

"Again. I realize that."

"I don't think you do." I grab her arm and she swerves the car a little. Maybe she's more freaked than she's letting on. I need to work that to my advantage.

"Bec." I soften my voice now. "He's. A. Kid."

"Yeah, well, so was my sister." Her eyes turn icy again and I can't help but feel her pain. "Please, please calm down," she pleads. "I'm just following your lead."

"What?" I ask, shocked again.

"You had the idea for the gun." She glances in my direction. "You were clever, Johnny. I upped my game as well with another idea for back-up—to help us get what we want. Some additional insurance. Don't you think that's wise?"

For the life of me, I can't remember how I fell for this asinine plan. But I desperately want it to be over so we can finally put all this to rest. Finally do something about Travis instead of all the talking. Talking. Talking. Talking.

We talked a lot in those first few weeks. I'd go the accident site and watch her work. She had all these theories and ideas. And when one didn't pan out, she'd move on to another. I started looking forward to going there, which was disturbing. But being around Becca helped. Sometimes we'd even talk about things not related to the accident. I told her about the colleges scouting me and my troubles with my grades. I told her how I thought I was letting Mom down.

"So I'll tutor you," she said, like it was the only logical solution.

"Becca, I'm getting D's in almost all of my classes," I said. "I don't need a tutor, I need a miracle."

"Same thing." She laughed.

"You really think you I could get my grades up to meet the college requirements?" Even my guidance counselor seemed to have lost hope.

"With my help? Yes, I do."

Damn, she was confident. Not in a cocky or conceded way; she was just so sure of herself. She made me believe it too.

I started to get excited until I realized there was a problem. One gigantic issue.

Money.

I had *nada*.

"I know a way you could work it off," she said.

"How?" I asked, willing to do just about anything.

"Help me make things right."

That's how we got started. It didn't seem evil or criminal at first. We were just looking for the person responsible for the accident. Investigating. Well, that's what I was doing. Becca? She was looking to prove what she already knew. That girl was always two steps ahead in everything she did. This was no different.

Once we had that proof? Well, that's when things began to change. That's when I began to get glimpse of what Becca was really capable of. She kept everything bottled up, but once we had a target—Travis—she let holy hell rain down.

She messed with him for almost a year. Started rumors about him on social media; used his account for her school lunches; reported him to the police for vandalism; placed him at the scene of another hit-and-run. Real detailed, calculated shit. Nothing stuck, but it raised suspicion.

At the time, I blamed it on her grief, on her parents, on anyone else I could besides Becca. But now there's no one left. And I'm so ready to finish this and be done with her games.

"Johnny." Becca gives me the softest kiss when we stop at the light. I wish I could ignore the effect it has on me, but I think my body will always respond to her. "Trust me, our opponent will be more responsive this way. We've captured his pawn."

"In what way will he be more responsive?" I bristle, the betrayal thick in my throat.

"We needed this leverage." She steals a glance at that leverage in the rearview mirror before accelerating. "Something, someone, he cares about. He'll know we're not messing around."

"So what's the plan with Travis then?" I ask, not daring to look in the backseat. It's the only way I can get through this. "How will we communicate with him?"

"Oh, we'll grab him too," she says, changing lanes.

"When?" My stomach turns, trying to process the new information.

"Tomorrow."

"Tomorrow? What are we going to do with the kid overnight? His parents will realize he's missing."

"Not if we get Travis to help cover for us," she says.

"Why would he do that?" I ask, not following.

"Because we have a hostage, dumbass," she snaps.

I wince at her words and slide farther toward my door, growing desperate for a way out.

Becca's expression softens as she moves a hand toward me. She knows that was a low blow. We have unwritten rules. She never insults my intelligence, and I never call attention to her overall social awkwardness. But everything is unraveling tonight.

"I'm sorry," she says. "I just can't take it when you don't trust me. I'm doing this for us, Johnny." The speedometer inches its way up.

"So tell me the plan then," I say, trying to talk her down. I'm up to the plate now and there's no going back—we're in too deep. And if we get pulled over, we're done.

Becca makes no move to fill me in.

I can't risk anymore surprises, so I nudge her along. "You're saying that by tomorrow we'll have *two* hostages?"

"Correct."

"Do you realize that will double the felony count if we're caught?" I ask. But I'm worried that maybe she doesn't care anymore. Maybe this is her endgame.

"Then we better not get caught." She shrugs, and I suddenly know, without a doubt, that I have no say whatsoever. This is the Becca show and I'm only here for the ride.

"Jesus, Becca." I bury my head in my hands, completely lost. "This is so fucked up."

"Fucked up?" she asks, her lips turning up in the corners. "Or brilliant? This is what we call increasing the odds."

Welcome to Hush

Responsible:

I did it because of love. Isn't that always the reason? In my case, unfortunately, I loved more. And that's not a good feeling. It's not equal, and there's nothing that feels worse than an imbalance. Luckily, I was willing to do almost anything to level the playing field. To get us on equal footing.

It's common sense. Basic math, really.

Though prediction, analysis, and statistics should not be mistaken for control.

I learned that the hard way.

17

....

BECCA

....

It wasn't easy to break up with Travis, especially being in lockdown. Not that I was there long. My parents had read something about increased suicide rates for twins who lose their other half; in reality, the findings from this supposed study said that the increase in suicide was really quite minuscule and the number of subjects included in the analysis was far too low to hold any validity. To use Brit's words, it was bunk. But my parents didn't care. When they found me in the fetal position in the special waiting room after my visit with Ethan, they thought I was having a breakdown and decided they weren't taking any chances with their remaining progeny.

It was either that or they simply couldn't deal with me.

What my parents didn't know, that day they dropped me off on the infamous fourth floor, was that I'd just dealt with a message from Brit's murderer. Something sure to make the most stable person snap. Unfortunately, or predictably, Ethan was nowhere to be found once Nurse Julie showed up. He (and his daisies) disappeared, so I looked like the delusional one.

For three days I sat in a semi-sedated state—sleeping, daydreaming, and plotting. Once the medication wore off, I vowed never to feel like that again. Out of control. I wouldn't let my *feelings* get the best of me again. I wasn't weak or stupid. I was driven. Determined. Focused. Yes, from that point forward, I'd hold on to my anger and use it to right all the wrongs, to make things even again. As Isaac Newton once said, "To every action there is always opposed an equal reaction." As I sat in that place where life and death fought every single second, I began to formulate my reaction.

Sadly, a hospital stay was nothing new for me. My parents were frequently concerned about my "behavior." I'd started seeing a psychiatrist when I was thirteen. It was just another thing that Brit convinced them to do, despite the fact that my little meltdowns always came after she'd screwed me over in some way. I was never good about handling her—never could manage it. My punishment? Psychiatric help.

"Rebecca," Mom would say, using my given name as she started one of her many speeches on the subject while I tried to conceal my laughter. As if using my full name would make me take her seriously.

"We know the bond between you and Brit is strong, but you have to remember that you are your own person," she'd say. Followed by, "Your worth isn't connected to your sister." And closing with, "You need to focus on yourself instead of being so worried about what Brit is doing all the time."

I'd heard various forms of that lecture over the years

and was forced to see the doctor whenever Mom thought it was time for a "tune-up." I can't blame her. After my first few sessions, the doctor tossed around all the key words that would put Mom on high alert. Words like "obsessive," "compulsive," "detached," "depressed," "anxious," and "narcissistic." Basically every parent's nightmare.

So I'd go to see the doctor to appease my mother. The result was always the same: inconclusive. My condition wasn't serious enough—or the doctor wasn't confident enough in her diagnosis—for medication, so the solution was talk therapy and group meetings. *That* was brutal enough, but after we lost Brit, we added all these sessions about surviving the loss of your twin. Even in death my sister continued to take center stage.

The sessions didn't last, and in the months that passed, my mental health became a fading issue in the Waters household. Simply getting through the day was the best we could hope for.

———

Once I was free from the Nut Hut, and my parents were off suicide watch, I went to work. First order of business? Terminating my relationship with Travis Kent.

I wanted him rattled. Looking back, I guess I could've stayed with him and let him think he had the upper hand before making a surprise attack that would shatter his world. Then I thought, *that would be too easy for this scum*. I wanted him worried, paranoid. I wanted him to get sloppy. That's why I took my time.

And it took some doing to break up with him—a little

legal work, if you will. He didn't go away easily. Not until that December day when I told him I had evidence that put him at the scene of the accident and I was going to the police with it.

He believed me.

When I went on to mention other little theories about his motive and opportunity, he panicked. He'd been through the court system enough times; he was fluent in legalese. He denied and backpedaled and made excuses like any guilty party would. This definitely was not the untouchable Travis Kent I'd come to know.

But then he had the nerve to threaten me. Well, let's just say that he shouldn't have done that.

"I'll tell them you were part of it," he said in the darkened corridor of the school where he used to steal me away for a kiss or touch—something he always needed more than I did. "That you were part of the whole thing."

"Doubt that'll work, since the only person who knew about us is dead." I chuckled, keeping a safe distance between us.

"It'll be my word against yours." He slammed his hand against the wall.

"You think that will work with your record?" I asked, unflinching. It was clear he hadn't thought it through.

"It may." He shrugged as he tried to regain his composure.

"Do you know how many of Brit's friends would testify against you? All I'll have to do is plant the seed. You were obsessed with her. You couldn't have her. You chased her off the road. The girls would eat it up."

"Do you know how many people I could get to say you hated your sister?" he countered.

It was either a standoff or a game. But one thing was certain—our relationship was over.

It was the first step.

Who would make the next move?

It didn't really matter to me. Point was, I was ready to play. And I always won.

18

The car ride is uncomfortable the rest of the drive. Ethan is still knocked out. I don't have a clue about the drug in the syringe. Becca said it was best to keep some details secret, in case something goes wrong and I have to talk to police. But what about Becca? How is she protected? Why didn't we talk about what she would do if questioned?

She pulls the car in as close as we can to our holding place—the ruins.

Detroit has become known for its abandoned homes and businesses, churches and schools, factories and shops. Some have been out of use for so long that they're being taken over by Mother Nature. Grass, plants, even trees have grown inside, around, and over the cement and wood and brick. It'd be pretty cool if it weren't so depressing. We call them the ruins. Yes, Detroit is the modern-day Rome, and Becca and I are modern-day gladiators fighting for our lives. Or maybe Ethan and Travis are, and Becca and I are just the cowards manipulating everything from the stands for our entertainment.

The ruins have many purposes in the city. The homeless, people down on their luck, and runaways squat in the open structures. Some people use the buildings to get extra cash, stripping them of anything of value—like copper piping, fixtures, furniture, you name it—and then selling off the pieces. I know of a few locations that are used for underground fighting events. But my favorite? High school parties. We've had some of the most epic benders in the larger spots—sometimes with live music.

And because the ruins are so popular, and some locations are really busy (or dangerous), Becca gave me the job of finding the place for our negotiations with Travis. Safe, remote, not too far from home . . . with a room where we could contain a person should his confession take longer than expected.

That was the gist of our entire plan. *Get Travis to confess.*

It was only a few weeks into our investigation when Travis Kent became a suspect. Becca told me that he'd been hooking up with Brit on the down-low. She also knew that her sister was trying to end it. That's where Brit was before the accident—at Travis Kent's home. Becca didn't tell me everything—she said she still felt obligated to protect Brit's privacy—but she was positive that Travis was to blame for the car wreck.

She said he'd threatened Brit all the time when they were together. She'd overheard him at the house. And after, she heard him bragging about it to one of his freaky gamer friends.

"I understand if you don't want to get involved," she said to me. "But I can't let my sister's killer walk free."

She had this accusing tone—as if she cared more about

losing her sister than I cared about losing my mom. I wasn't having it.

"And I won't let my mother's killer walk, either," I countered.

So began our pact to make Travis Kent pay.

"You should take the pawn over there," Becca says now, shaking me from my memory.

Of course, he's not Ethan to her. He's just the pawn.

I know what she's trying to do, but holding this kid at a distance isn't going to work. Not for me.

She points from Ethan to the streetlamp. "It's time to send a message to our opponent. The game has begun."

I open the door to the backseat and slide my arms under Ethan's pits, dragging him out of the car. He's about his brother's height. Tall for a middle school kid, but scrawny under his bulky sweatshirt. His head plops back and rests on his shoulder and I can't help but stare. No visible Adam's apple on his exposed neck and not a trace of stubble on his skin. He's still a boy—an overstretched baby.

I set him down by the light and prop him up per Becca's instructions.

My heart squeezes in my chest. This is so wrong. I wonder what I would do to somebody if they did the same thing to Cassie. But I know I can't go there right now. We are simply doing what we have to do. It's what I keep telling myself. *It's just a game. Only a game.*

Yet the battered face and bruised body that's currently leaning up against the lamppost tells a very different story.

We've stopped here because we need light, and Becca wants to alert Travis. But I want to delay as long as possible. Where we're going next is anything but pleasant.

"Christ, what's that smell?" I ask, trying not to dry heave.

"Urine and feces," Becca answers easily. Unaffected. "I'm sure the pawn defecated on himself during our struggle. It's pretty common in this type of situation."

The fact that she'd know this makes me go cold.

"Here," she says, handing me the newspaper. "Just like we planned to do with Travis."

We planned to document everything with Travis. Take photos with dates—mark the moment when we took him hostage—in case we needed it later. Now, even though our hostage has changed, the plan has not.

Holding my breath, I unfold today's newspaper, rest it on Ethan's chest, and take a photo with the untraceable prepaid cellphone we picked up a few weeks ago.

I hold out the phone and show the photo to Becca. She nods, so I take the newspaper off Ethan's chest, make sure he still has a pulse, and sling him up over my shoulder. We have to walk now.

Becca shines the light in my path so I can see where I'm going. I raise my eyes to the sky instead, hoping to see Anna's Star. Though I know it wouldn't guide me in this direction. It would point me in the direction to get my ass straight home. Shit. Mom would be so ashamed if she could see me now.

I slow my pace, almost expecting to hear a crack of thunder. I think we're making the Gods very angry tonight.

Before I met Becca, I never committed a crime. Not one. No drugs, underage drinking, or speeding tickets. No truancy, assault, or vandalism. I never even pocketed a stick of Laffy Taffy from the gas station like everyone else did back in middle school before the Friday night football games.

As we walk, I tick off the offenses one by one. I've counted a minimum of ten—most of them felonies. Several involving a freaking thirteen-year-old. And if they figure it out, I'll be charged as an adult and put away for the rest of my life. No question.

Still, I let Becca lead. Maybe because that's how it's always been with us. Maybe because this plan has let me escape what's really happening in my life. The ultimate distraction. Maybe because doing *something* feels better than doing *nothing*.

It's like I'm under some kind of spell. Like the way the Manson family followed Charles. Or the way Clyde supposedly followed Bonnie. Or like that one woman in Canada who helped her husband kidnap and kill those girls.

Love can make monsters out of us. Or is it despair? Whatever it is, it works. I don't feel like me anymore. I feel like I've been swallowed up by a darkness that I never knew was inside. It's a terrifying place to be—so bad, I'll do anything to escape it.

Even continue down the hill to follow Becca's light.

19

BECCA

Executing—*executing, ha ha!*—a plan like mine required a lot of work. And time. It clearly wasn't for the faint of heart, or for those looking for the instant gratification most of us thrive on.

It was about precision, details, sacrifice. I'd learn it would also take nerves of steel to pull off, especially as my game plan adapted and changed, taking on a life of its own. Originally, the objective of the game was to sic the police on Travis.

He'd given me a lot of evidence on his own: his newly painted Jeep with a huge dent that had been cheaply repaired; a sketchy attendance record after the accident; a history of trouble with the law; and swarms of rumors about his general "freakiness" in school.

What I needed was evidence linking him to the site (because I'd lied when I told him I had it); witnesses to back up the motive that he was obsessed with Brit; and an enhanced rap sheet.

I started with the rap sheet, framing him for petty crimes

and even accusing him of causing another accident. I knew it wouldn't amount to anything, but just having it recorded would help our case.

Next up was to plant evidence at the crash site. My car and the Vegas' car had already been totaled and hauled away before I could use them. But I did get a very nice new vehicle out of the deal. Brit's one parting gift. Thanks, sis.

I spent days combing over the site with Johnny to find something to link Travis to it; there was nothing to be had. He'd covered his tracks. That's when I had to go out on my own. I needed to do a little creative detective work to make it happen, but Johnny couldn't know about that part. For this to work, his hatred of Travis had to be genuine. And justified.

Once I got going, it wasn't hard. One day, in the school parking lot, I was able to crack Travis's side mirror and remove a piece of glass that could be transferred to the site, as well as a chunk of rust from the front end of his Jeep. Then I added a candy wrapper and some other garbage with his fingerprints on it that "must've fallen out of his car when he got out to assess the damage."

Now close to the next step—of adding my witnesses to the mix—I was giddy to bust him. But when I looked at the punishment for manslaughter according to Michigan law, I wasn't impressed. Twelve years looked about the average, and that was only if we were lucky enough to get a guilty verdict. It wasn't nearly long enough.

A new plan was necessary—one with more pain and the prison time he deserved. That's when I decided to capture and sedate Travis and force a confession we could take to the police.

But his confession couldn't *look* forced; that was key. We'd have to get it without the risk of him recanting his story and without any opportunity for him to implicate me.

So the chess match began.

Travis didn't stand a chance. I'd been playing since I was eight years old: the logic and symmetry had always appealed to me. My new objective, to quote Bobby Fischer, was to "crush the opponent's mind."

I knew exactly how to accomplish just that. All I had to do was gather my pieces.

───────────

With my new plan in place, I needed access to medication. Sedatives for the confession and holding period and something to end it all, if things went awry. *Always have a back-up.*

I had the perfect solution: a volunteer position at the hospital. Nurse Julie got me the job.

The first day, Julie took me on a tour around her floor—the second floor. "I'm so glad you're doing this, Becca. It's going to be really good for you."

She had no idea.

"Thank you," I said. "I'm happy to be here."

She put her arm around my shoulder and I bit the inside of my lip so I wouldn't groan. I turned up the corners of my mouth to form something that resembled a smile. It was an expression passed down from my father—one that showed up whenever I talked about college.

"You're going to do splendidly wherever you land, Becca,"

he'd say before flashing his grimace. My poor father. He knew I was going to go further with my education than he ever had, and it brought him pain just to think about it. And my parents wondered where the narcissism came from.

That first night at the hospital, I served as an errand girl. Anything the nurses needed, I was at their command. Julie gave me pink scrubs, no doubt an homage to the old candy striper days.

Though I hated pink, I didn't mind the job.

Make copies of these forms: check.

Clean the waiting area and make coffee: check.

Bring flowers to room 208 and 213: sure thing.

As I did it all, with a smile, I took notice of everything: the number of rooms on the floor; where the patient information was kept; the amount of staff on a shift; the comings and goings in the medication room; and the time when nurses started divvying out evening drugs. That last piece of information was of particular interest to me.

After the accident and my discharge from the Nut Hut, I spent all my free time at the crash site, the hospital, and in my room studying pharmaceuticals. Oh, the things I learned. It's true it took a lot longer than expected; anything worthwhile usually does.

Several months later, when I was finally ready, I set out to pocket the medication. It worked surprisingly well. Time consuming but effective. After watching the entire process of gathering, distributing, and disposing the drugs, I found a few chinks in the system and used them in various ways.

One afternoon, I wanted to test the theory. I walked

into a room with a vase of bright tulips as a cover. As the medication was administered to Motorcycle Man, a twenty-something guy who was recovering from a nasty accident, I created a diversion. I bumped into the nurse's medication cart on my way to set the vase on the windowsill. As I helped steady the cart, I swapped out the real medication with a used vial that I'd refilled with saline. At that point, I had already decided that an injectable would work the best.

Earlier, I'd found a way to get the used vials before they made it into the Sharps Container. Like I said, it was a slow-going mission, but I eventually had what I needed.

Motorcycle Man missed his evening dose of pain meds that day. I wasn't too worried. If the patients complained enough, they could always get extra. He'd be fine.

If not? Well, what can I say? Sacrifice for the greater good.

Next came mastering the skill of injecting my chosen drug. That's where the nerves of steel came into play. I got my hands on the syringes but had no idea how to use them. It only took a few online tutorials from a library computer to remedy that problem.

I took the first plunge on my pillow, before moving on to Brit's old stuffed animals, bananas, and a raw chicken breast.

The final test? A real human being.

Now I'm sure I could have roped in a volunteer from my ASP group, all in the name of learning, but I couldn't risk it. I was alone in this and I would have to use my own body as a pincushion.

As I got closer to the date of my plan to make Travis pay, I spent a few evenings locked in my bedroom playing nurse. The first targets were my arms and legs. It wasn't that bad, as long as I didn't look when the needle met my skin. The last of the jabs involved a bit more preparation—and by preparation, I mean swigs of Dad's brandy—because the last target was my neck. I fainted the first time I did it.

Needles used to make me queasy. Even the proper name, "hypodermic needle," was cringe-worthy. The stainless-steel tube was sterile and chilling, and the longer the needle, the worse it was. But I guess all medical equipment can be unnerving. Tools for the body that can be used to repair or destroy never seem quite right. The part of the needle that really made my stomach roll was the tip, beveled in a sharp point. And the way you flick the syringe before drawing out the medication, letting one lonely drop hang from that beveled point. It made my mouth fill.

Yet despite my aversion to the instrument, I learned to respect it.

There was something satisfying about the way it felt in my hand as the sharp tip of the needle punctured the skin, sinking into the epidermis. That popping sensation as it penetrated the body.

It didn't take me long to become proficient at injecting.

My plan was in full motion. Even so, the sight of Travis would sway me from time to time. If only temporarily. I'd see him in school, walking down the hall at a pace always a few seconds faster than most students. A few seconds that set him apart. His muscular arms swaying with each step. Arms that used to swoop out from the dark corners of the school to grab me at random times during the day so he could put his mouth on me. It was those memories that left me uncertain. At times I thought I may have to stop.

Until I remembered Brit.

That's all it took to get right again.

I continued to work at the hospital long after my lessons were over, moving to entertainment on the children's floor. I liked being there and, even more, I enjoyed the look I'd get when I told people. It was one of admiration and respect. I recognized that look because Brit was once on the receiving end of it all the time.

It was just one more thing I'd stolen from her.

20

JOHNNY

. . . .

I knew I was falling for Becca about a month after she started tutoring me. We spent a lot of time studying together—I was so behind—and sometimes I talked her into picking me up on the weekends so we could hang out at the coffee shop.

She knew about my messed-up brain. And she knew all kinds of tricks to help me make it work better. She said she understood what it was like to think differently—she believed it's what made us extraordinary. *We're the lucky ones*, she said.

Sometimes, I'd ask Becca about her sister and tell her about Mom. That's how our friendship began—wallowing in our pain. But it soon grew to something much more. And one day, she opened up to me—more than she'd ever done before.

She'd looked nervous all day at school, but of course wouldn't tell me what was bothering her. Then, after last bell, she called out to me while I was gathering my things at my locker.

"Johnny," she yelled out. It was the first time I'd ever

heard her raise her voice. That did something to me; I'm not sure why. It could've been because she never liked to call attention to herself. That was Brit's role—attention seeker. And Becca seemed to be content with hers—wallflower.

"Hey, what's up?" I asked as she sped over to me, out of breath and all flush-faced. It was then that I noticed, really noticed, just how beautiful she was. Of course, I always thought she was hot in an understated sort of way. But like this—excited, lively, and happy to see me—she took my breath away.

Her hand slid into her coat pocket, like she was trying to steady it. She wore this tweed blazer—a man's blazer, I'm pretty sure. She wore that thing over everything. Her smart oxford shirts. Her less-smart but more impressive tank tops. And, if she was feeling funky, she'd wear it over her Wonder Woman tee.

That didn't quite fit… though I'm sure she loved Wonder Woman. Who wouldn't? But wearing anything commercial like that was not her deal. I later found out it'd been Brit's.

She seemed stronger when she wore it.

"Would you want to come with me today after school?" she asked, the nerves back.

"Where to?" I said, upbeat, light, hoping it'd make her less nervous.

"The hospital. I do some work with kids there," she said.

Thinking back, I realized she did always have something to do on Tuesdays, but she'd always been mysterious about it. I absolutely had to know more.

"Sure," I agreed, and off we went.

While Becca was getting settled in, I ran into Ava's mom, Rita, at the nurses' station.

"What are you doing here, Johnny Vega?" she asked, wrapping me in a hug. "Are the girls with you?"

"No, it's just me."

Rita usually worked with the psych patients on the fourth floor. My mom and Rita had become fast friends once it was out that Cass and Ava were together. Mom thought it'd be a great idea to have me talk to Rita about psych work. It was really one of my only interests in school, and if I was going to play college ball, I'd need a major.

It was actually a great idea.

"I'm here with my girlfriend," I told her. "She volunteers with the kids."

"Rebecca Waters?" Rita asked in a strange voice. She was either shocked or bothered, I couldn't tell which. Poor Bec; she rubs a lot of people the wrong way.

"That's the one," I said, and she nodded.

"How's your dad doing these days?" Rita changed the subject.

"He's hanging in there," I said, and then Becca came out of one of the rooms and waved me over. "Ah, looks like I have to go."

"Oh, okay." Rita looked disappointed. "Take care of yourself, kiddo," she said before I made my way to Bec.

We spent about an hour with the kids, and they were pretty great. I'm not going to lie—they didn't come up and hug Becca or squeal when she arrived—but many of them, especially the smart, shy ones, looked up when she walked in. And though they were slow to warm, they started making their way to her table—where she sat with her puzzles and Legos and crosswords. It was a blast to watch.

I remember the way Becca looked up at me and smiled that day. I lost it. She'd smiled at me before, but never like this. It had never really reached her eyes before. She was always so reserved, and her displays of emotion were so few and far between, that an honest-to-goodness smile from Bec was like a rare gift.

I wanted more.

We finished up with the kids and walked out to the hall, when I stopped her. I couldn't help it. I pulled her into a private nook by the elevator and moved in slowly, afraid she'd back away. That's how she always felt to me, just out of my reach. We'd already gotten our first kiss out of the way and were growing slightly more comfortable around each other; it was time to make my next move.

I watched her chest rise and fall as she took quick shallow breaths. It made her boobs bounce in the most fantastic way and drove me insane, so I just went for it. I brushed my lips against hers, prepared for her to shut me down.

She didn't.

Instead, she followed my lead. Searing her lips to mine. Teasing me with her tongue. It was a surprise. A fucking awesome one. She smelled like girl shampoo, all clean and sweet, and she tasted like orange baby aspirin, because she was always popping those vitamin C tablets anytime we were around people.

I deepened the kiss and pushed into her... until I got hard. I shifted my hips so I wouldn't freak her out.

There was no need to worry. She reached out and linked her fingers in my belt loops, pushing all her right parts onto my raging hard-on. We had completely forgotten that we were in public.

This went on for some time and I realized I'd better shut it the hell down before we got hauled out of there like a bunch of perverts.

"I liked that," she said when I pulled away to look at her.

"I liked that, too," I agreed.

"You know, this is the first time I've been with a boy who Brit didn't pick out for me."

"What do you mean?"

"Brit always set me up on dates. I don't think I would've ever been on one without her. In case you haven't noticed, I'm not exactly a people person."

I couldn't help but laugh at the way she'd just blurt these things out. It also helped defuse the situation I had going on below the belt.

"I'm serious."

"Sorry, Bec. I know you are."

"Even here, the kids always gravitate toward the cheerleaders, the happy people, all bubbly and fun—like you. They really just tolerate me."

"What are you talking about? The kids love you."

"The ones who are like me, maybe. But I really like them all."

"I can tell," I said.

"It's their minds. Common sense hasn't kicked in yet, and they still think everything is possible. They don't have to pretend or hide who they really are because they're not worried about being judged or not fitting in yet." There was so much pain in her voice—I had no idea she even cared what other people thought. She just always seemed like her own island to me. Happy and content to be on her own.

"Do you worry about that?" I asked her. "Fitting in? Being judged?"

"Of course. I'm not a robot," she deadpanned, in a voice that sounded very much like a robot.

It made me grin. The odd couple, we were.

"You fit in, Bec," I told her, kissing her one more time. "You fit with me."

Becca had spent a lot of time at the hospital even *before* she started volunteering. She was there for Brit. Unlike Mom, Brit didn't die at the scene. It took a month before the Waters family decided to pull the plug. Becca stayed there the entire time.

She'd roam the floors. All the time, watching. Watching the docs, the nurses, the patients. Of course, Becca already knew Brit was gone. I'm sure she understood every word when the surgeon showed the family the brain scan. Becca's a person of logic, science, numbers—not hope. I think she started devising the plan then, even before Brit was gone.

If it wasn't for the kids and her volunteer work with them—calculated or not—I don't think she would've made it.

Those kids helped bring her back to life. And she really cared for them, I know she did. She could've found something else as a front; she could've spent a lot less time there. But she didn't.

That's why it doesn't make sense that she'd take Travis's brother. He's young, and more importantly, he's innocent in this whole thing. Looking at her now, it's hard to believe she's the same girl I watched at the hospital that day.

She's become cold, hard, and freaking frightening. It's making me second-guess everything. Is it possible that she was pretending with those kids for my benefit? Part of her plan to reel me in? Am I the other pawn in her game?

I can't help but wonder if I've been played all along.

21

BECCA

....

I n the beginning, I went to the accident site to get a sense of what really happened. To figure out how Travis had pulled it off. I continued going there to plant evidence against him. Of course, I soon realized I needed more; the only way I'd get my justice was if he confessed.

Back when I was re-creating the accident scene to make my theory sound believable, I took measurements and worked out equations for the speed and location of the cars on impact, and did some trajectory-based analysis. It wasn't accurate, only an educated guess. There were a few skid marks left of the road at that time, but nothing that screamed foul play. The police had chalked it up to an accident. But Travis didn't have to know that.

The crash site was in a fairly isolated area, so I had the privacy I needed for my work.

When I finally confronted Travis, he never really did confirm or deny his part in all of it. But I knew. I ran that last conversation with my sister through my mind, over and over again: "That little psycho is following me," she'd said. In that moment, Brit had told me all I needed to know.

Even when I wasn't investigating, I went to the site because I could think better out there. It was almost as if I could feel my sister. I knew it was metaphysical garbage, but at the time, I needed something.

Because of the deep, deep hole.

I lived in there. In darkness. Going through the motions of my life in a haze. The only thing that made sense was seeing that justice was done. But as I worked through how I'd make Travis pay, I was missing something. Someone. I needed another person to pull it off. There was no other way around it.

Then something amazing happened. Johnny Vega started showing up.

"What are you doing here?" I asked him one afternoon, recognizing his face (it was a good face) from the baseball posters in school. I'd reviewed the stats on occasion. Baseball was a mathematician's sport—statistics and equations galore.

He was on foot. Alone.

"What are *you* doing here?" He answered my question with a question. One of my biggest pet peeves, but I let it go because he didn't look so good.

When he offered his condolences, I wasn't surprised. Surely a guy like Johnny knew my sister.

"Thanks," I said, saying his name softly in my mind. *Johnny Vega.*

It clicked.

The police report immediately came to mind: *Anna Vega pronounced dead at the scene.* Until that very moment, I had never once thought about the other driver. I knew about her, surely. And that was it. I didn't put her family's loss with ours; I didn't think of her that way. She was just a casualty of the accident.

Johnny shifted, from his left foot to his right. I realized why he was here. He was mourning his mother, and from the look of it, he had been for quite some time.

He was a gift—the answer to everything. He could help.

I looked over my prize. His dark hair was unkempt, flattened in areas, puffed out in others. It reminded me of the bumpy road we were standing on. He wore a navy track jacket and black jeans that hung off him, puddling at his ankles, though it looked more like weight loss than a fashion statement. He was fairly clean-cut. Most of the athletes in school were. Dark circles shadowed his eyes, distracting from his otherwise flawless face.

I don't think I'd ever spent so much time looking at someone—trying to figure them out. But I quickly knew that if this was going to work, I'd need to know everything about him. So I took out my tape measure and notebook—I still had them in my bag—and I started measuring things and writing things. I took notes from all angles and wrote my equations down on paper. He wouldn't be able to resist asking questions.

I felt his eyes on me, trying to understand what I was doing out here.

"What are you doing?" he finally asked.

"Investigating," I said, pretending to be preoccupied.

"The accident?" he asked.

I nodded, still messing with my tape measure.

"Why?"

"Because I don't think it was an accident."

Boom!

"First of all, the skid marks on the road don't seem to match the police report," I began. "It looks like my sister swerved up there." I pointed. "Not down here at the point of impact."

I continued reading off my mental script, the same story I'd given Travis. I was so focused on my delivery that I missed the cues. The signal that he was going to vomit.

So he was a little weak, then.

Good to know. Good to know.

Johnny had turned to the side and heaved up his lunch. He looked apologetic, like it was his fault his body betrayed him.

I handed him a tissue from my bag. Waiting just a min-ute or two to let him recover, I jumped back to the task at hand. I had him on the edge and it was time to lure him in.

"What? It hasn't crossed your mind?" I asked.

He shrugged.

Hmm. Doesn't question things.

"Don't you think the circumstances surrounding the accident are odd?" I asked.

"What do you mean by odd?"

Needs things spelled out.

"Suspect?" I offered.

"What are you saying?" he asked, his jaw tightening with each word.

"I'm saying it wasn't an accident, as I mentioned when

you first started grilling me," I said, and I went back to my note-taking.

Then he started pushing me with more questions. He wanted details. That was a promising sign.

In the weeks ahead, I kept Johnny on a need-to-know basis. Giving him bits and pieces of information that kept his suspicions up, kept him hungry for more. We spent the rest of the time sitting on the side of the road, talking. I learned that's what he responded to most of all—our conversations. He craved it.

To keep moving forward, I needed ammunition. I needed to know how to get a boy to do my bidding, so I went into Brit's arsenal. She always had them eating from her tiny hand.

I used it all. From the overplayed hard-to-get, to unwavering attention, Johnny ate it up. Occasionally I'd throw him a bone with a touch, a smile, or a flash of the eyes that hinted toward something wicked.

It worked.

The Elements of a Crime:
#2 Conduct

Conduct *(actus reus)* refers to the objective element of a crime. *Actus reus* is the Latin term for "guilty act." When a *guilty act* and *guilty mind* are proven together, beyond a reasonable doubt, it equates to criminal liability. So for *actus reus* to occur, there has to have been a criminal act—a bodily movement, voluntary or involuntary.

So, you ask, was there a bodily movement—a guilty act—for me?

Yeah, you could say there was definitely one of those.

There were a few of them, actually.

And when those acts were done, I watched someone die.

One minute, I had someone's life in my hands. The next, I stood by as it slipped away.

22

JOHNNY

I carry Ethan down the hill to our designated place. His breathing is deep, his body completely pliant, draped over my shoulder. Becca shines the light on the path. Actually, it's not really a path. We've been down here several times before to get the room ready, but we always park in a different place and walk there using a new route.

I take baby steps downward, shifting my weight to balance Ethan on my shoulder. He smells better now—after Becca changed his pants like a goddamn baby. I wonder if this is what she had in mind when she told me to add a change of clothes to my list.

Becca is always one step ahead of everyone. Cunning, I guess you'd call her. Everything is calculated and planned out to the last detail. And she's so confident, you can't help believe whatever she says. Following her ... it's easy.

We walk into the dank, moldy building. We chose the old library because it's secluded and hard to get to due to the fact that the nearby parking lot is caved in. From the outside, most of the structure has held together, but inside, it's crumbling. The only way to get down here is to walk down a steep hill.

I haul the younger Kent brother inside. We walk along the decaying walls and over the piles of books still scattered all over the floor. I can't help think about the irony—our story is definitely novel-worthy.

There's one tiny room in the building—must've been for the librarian or office workers—that's still intact. Ceiling, floor, four walls, and a door.

After I'd brought Becca out here and she approved, we came back out to reinforce the door with locks and such.

I place Ethan on the bed. My arms tighten as I lower him down, careful not to drop him too hard. Becca goes to work on his restraints. After he's all nice and secure, she gives him another dose of drugs and closes the door.

I rest my head on it.

When a whimper comes from the other side, I reach for the doorknob.

Becca's hand clamps down over mine.

"You can't let him see us, Johnny," Becca spits. "No witnesses. We leave him. The rope is long enough for him to grab water and food. And he can reach the bucket in the corner. I'm sorry, but this is the way it has to be. The new dose will kick in soon anyway. It should carry him until the morning."

Ethan's voice rings out in the decaying space. It's high and sounds like gibberish, but if I strain I know he's calling for his mommy. It cuts right through my gut.

I don't blame him for it. You always hear about people—even the toughest gangsters or soldiers—calling for their mother when in danger or facing death. It's natural. Innate. That is what Ethan is doing right now. And while I hope he's not really in that kind of danger at our hands, I can't be sure what direction Becca's going to lead us. All I know for sure is that we're stuck in this until tomorrow.

Suddenly, I want to call out for my mommy.

I look through the door, unable to help myself. We put a reverse peephole in so we could monitor Travis and freak him out when needed during our interrogation. There are actual manuals online that teach interrogation techniques. We were quick studies. After careful consideration, we opted out of the Guantanamo-style waterboarding and decided on some more psychological mind-fucking instead.

I watch as Ethan struggles. He's now strapped to the bed—one arm and one leg. We purchased state-of-the-art confinements, also found online. Becca set up a post office box, used various names, and paid with those advance-type debit cards. She ordered everything online and had it delivered. It wasn't hard.

Girl could be a master criminal if she wanted to be. I would never want to be on her bad side.

Ethan's balled up in a pile—his head tipped back and his lower lip twitching. But his breathing is still deep. He has a few minutes in this hell hole before he dozes again. I can see him slowly slipping away.

Becca is messing with the pre-paid cell phone—contacting Travis or working some part of the plan, no doubt.

"What are you going to tell him?" I ask. Taking Ethan

wasn't impulsive, so I'm sure she's just working the steps at this point.

"I'm using the gambling angle," she says.

During our stalking, we discovered that Travis has a lot of enemies. Not only does he game, he gambles. And he doesn't exactly have the best reputation in the inner circles.

"I'm a disgruntled player and I know he's been cheating," Becca says. "I'm demanding he gives me my money back or his brother pays the price."

Poor Ethan. I can't take my eyes off the kid.

We set up the place with battery-operated lighting we bought from a camping outfitter. Very important to see during an interrogation. Now I'm glad we have the light for Ethan.

There's this piece of skin hanging from his face. It must be from when he slammed into the wall in his struggle with Becca. His flesh must've caught on the brick. The end of the skin wiggles when he moves. I'm glued to my spot watching him … just watching.

"Jesus, Becca," I say as we walk to the car. "I didn't sign up for this! It was supposed to be a one-night job."

"Things change, Johnny."

"No. Not things. You. You've changed, and you're cutting me out of this entire operation. And now you expect me to be okay leaving this kid in here. It's twisted."

"I'm not trying to cut you out," she says, reaching out to stop me. "I knew if I told you that you'd get cold feet and you wouldn't want to finish what we started."

She's right about that.

Becca lets out a long sigh, clearly getting frustrated with

me. Then she swallows and tries again. "The probability of Travis escalating, doing something even bigger than causing an accident that killed two people, is about 90 percent. Potentially higher if he continues not to get caught. The question isn't whether there will be a next time. The question is when will be the next time."

Strange. I'm beginning to wonder the same thing about Becca. What will *she* do the next time someone crosses her? What will *I* do? We've already gone so far over the line of what's right, I don't know how we could go back.

Becca doesn't wait for my response to her argument. She continues on, even more committed than before.

"He needs to be brought to justice," she says, accentuating each word. "For himself. For us. For our families. I know how cruel it seems to take Ethan, but we're saving lives here. We're the good guys. Just remember that."

But can you, Becca? Can you?

I know I should walk out on this plan. Let Ethan go. Tell Becca to go to hell. But something holds me there and I do what I always do. I go along with it. Conscience be damned.

We drive home and my leg bounces up and down to a little beat. I've now chewed my lip raw. Becca rest her hand right above my knee and squeezes. Typically, I'd be thrilled by any sign of affection from my girl. Right now it only sickens me.

As she pulls into my driveway she says, "I'll handle everything with Travis. You don't have to be involved at all. I'll check on the pawn tomorrow before school to make sure he's okay."

"The pawn," I repeat. "Nice touch, by the way. So what

do you call me when nobody's listening? *Right Hand, Slackie, Slave*? Oh, I know: *Accomplice*?"

"I think that'd be the other way around, don't you?" Her brows are all knitted together as she faces me.

"How do get that?"

"Oh no you don't, Johnny. Now that we're in deep, you're going to start blaming me? You are the one who came up with this entire revenge plot."

"What are you talking about?"

She laughs. "*Let's make him pay. I won't let him walk around free after what he did. I'll get a gun.* Ring any bells?"

It does, but the memories are jumbled, and that makes me even queasier.

"Now's not the time for selective memory. You're in this, Johnny. I can carry most of the load, but you have to help me. You just help me get him to our next point. Help me get him where he needs to be. Help me get the confession and then we're done."

"Where *does* Travis need to be?" I ask, desperate to be done. "And when?"

"Tomorrow evening. I'll take you to the new location and we can work it all out after school."

I'm now suspiciously on the outside of this plan, though I wonder if I ever really was a participant or have always just been Becca's bitch. The serious doubt is beginning to kick in. Not just about this last hiccup but the whole thing. What the hell am I doing anyway? It could be a blessing that I haven't been as involved—I could go to the cops right now. I could make a deal and bargain for my life.

These thoughts come to a halt when I catch the way Becca's looking at me. It's like she can see right through me. She knows what I'm doing—the second-guessing. She can sense the betrayal.

"This is why I did what I did," she whispers, looking almost hurt.

I want to believe she is. That she actually feels. But that's the thing about Becca; there's always something off.

"You always need a back-up because people will turn on you the first chance they get," she says, and I know she's referring to me.

My stomach squeezes in on itself.

"Oh, and it's love, by the way." She wraps her arms around herself and looks up at me.

"Love?" I ask, confused.

"The name I call you by when nobody's listening," she says, going right for the jugular before turning away.

23

Travis was watching me, like any worthy opponent would. I saw him, lurking there on the blurred periphery edges of my daily life. He watched Johnny too. I had no choice but to get to work... and fast. Still, I couldn't afford any mistakes. I had to be stay steps ahead.

In this chess match, everyone in our world played a part. I thought of Ethan as the pawn, Cassie and Ava as the knight and bishop. The rook was Johnny—the protector, but also the piece that was most powerful in the endgame. The king represented my family, which left the most important piece of any game (the queen) to me, so I could *crush my opponent's mind.*

I started tutoring Johnny in exchange for his help. He was the key to my new plan. The only way I could go up against Travis.

I got the better end of my deal with Johnny, though. I enjoyed tutoring him; it wasn't hard. He wasn't a lost cause like so many teachers had thought throughout the years. He just had what *they'd* call a few learning disabilities. Personally,

I liked the way his brain worked. I liked a lot of things about him.

One afternoon, we were at his kitchen table working on basic geometry—complementary and supplementary angles. It was rudimentary material that Johnny just couldn't master.

He was particularly anxious, rocking in his chair, watching me instead of the equation I was writing on paper. Like he had all this energy pulsing inside him and it needed to be released. But he no longer had the dark circles under his eyes and his pants weren't quite so baggy anymore. He was the picture of health. Poreless olive skin, bright eyes, and a body that was so tight and strong you could bounce thousands of quarters off him. I admired that discipline.

He inched closer; his warm breath tickled my neck, my ear.

It was the moment I was waiting for. I tipped my head toward him, with what I hoped was a dreamy expression. Guys eat that up, apparently.

I didn't have to do this with Travis. He knew I was prickly and couldn't flirt to save my life. He also knew how to press my buttons and how to get me to sleep with him.

At least I was being myself while it happened.

With Johnny, every step had to be strategic. Each move made me more like Brit and less like me.

I fluttered my lashes, and that did it. He finally made his move.

Johnny tilted his head, ran a finger along my cheek, and leaned in. I met him halfway. His lips brushed along mine, slow and soft. It was like nothing I ever experienced. None of the sloppiness I had with Josh or the hard and fast moves with Travis. It was gentle and all-encompassing.

My eyes closed on their own, and that only increased the sensation of his lips on mine. I went taut and loose all at the same time—wound tight on the inside, but growing slack on the outside. My brain and body battled it out while he leisurely explored my mouth.

He was practiced, taking my bottom lip into his mouth before changing angles of the kiss. I lost my resolve to be in charge of this moment. Not that Johnny cared one way or another. He didn't care about being in control; he just wanted to feel.

Johnny was reviving me, bit by bit, bringing me back to the land of the living. It wasn't long before it started turning into more.

I shouldn't have let it happen. Johnny was just a piece on a board, helping me get to the endgame. I knew better than to let him in. Unfortunately, it was too late, and that was going to make everything more difficult.

24

Dad is passed out on the couch when I get home. The bottle is empty, but the lingering scent of booze still floats in the air. Cassie is in her room and comes out to join me in the living room when she hears the door close.

"What's going on?" she asks.

"Nothing," I say, nonchalantly scanning my body for any signs of our crime. "Back from hanging out at Becca's."

"Come here," she says, leading me to her room.

I follow and she closes the door behind us.

"I have something to tell you, Johnny," she starts. "Something we should've told you a long time ago, but we thought it'd be okay."

"Who is we?" I ask, hoping on everything that she doesn't know what I'm up to.

"Me, Ava, Rita."

"Rita?"

"Yes." She closes her eyes. "And she could be in deep shit if this gets out. So you have to promise this stays between us."

"Okay."

"I'm serious, Johnny. She could lose her job."

"Fine, I'll keep my mouth shut. What's it about?"

"Becca," she answers. "It's a long story, but you need to know. Are you ready?"

"Now that you've officially scared the crap out of me, yes, I'm ready. Tell me."

"First, let me say that when you first got together with Becca, I was thrilled," Cass begins. "After Mom died, you were so distant. I needed you so badly, but you were just gone. It felt like we'd lost you in the accident too. But then Becca started to make you happy. You were like the old you again. I talked about it all the time, but Ava never could join in on my enthusiasm. She even went so far as to warn me about Becca. She'd *heard* some things, she said. Well, you know how I feel about all that gossip bullshit."

I nodded, waiting for her to go on.

"So I made Ava tell me exactly what she knew. Turns out, the person she heard things from was her mom. You know, Rita has some pretty good stories from work—you can imagine the kinds of things she sees in her job."

"Of course," I say, growing impatient with the long setup.

"Well, she'd tell Ava a story about work once in a while, but she'd never use names. Until Becca."

"What do you mean, until Becca?"

"Turns out Becca has been to the Nut Hut a few times."

My stomach starts churning, the same way it did when Bec first told me Mom's accident wasn't an accident. I prepare for a quick dash to the bathroom just in case.

"Her first visit was probably the worst," Cass continues. "Apparently Becca completely melted down when their family cat disappeared a few years back and her parents didn't know what to do. She wouldn't eat or sleep, so they brought her in."

"Well, that's understandable," I say. "She takes loss pretty hard."

"Yeah, it was understandable. At first the docs thought it was grief and depression, but in later sessions they grew to find out it was more. She would tell them the cat was bad, and it was a good thing the cat had died because he liked Brit more than he liked her. And in her belongings, they found the cat's I.D. tag on her bracelet."

"Okay, that's all weird, but—"

"The charm had blood on it."

"What does that mean?" I ask, knowing the answer. Knowing what she's getting at.

"Rita has taken care of her a few other times. She's scared shitless of that girl. Once she found out that Becca went to our school, she warned Ava. And once you started dating her, Ava warned me."

"But I thought you both liked her," I say, unable to process this information.

"We did," she says. "We do. Actually, I wasn't too concerned. I thought maybe it was a misunderstanding. Plus, Becca isn't an easy person to like. But Rita told us that lately, her parents have been calling about permanent options for Becca—like medication, inpatient therapy, or some kind of center to send her to. Rita is really worried about you but she can't say anything. I've been watching Becca, and it's like she's taking a turn for the worse or something. I don't trust her."

Cass looks at me, but I say nothing.

"Does any of this make sense to you?" she asks. "Are you seeing it?"

"I think it's just the grief," I lie.

"Do you want me to talk to her?"

"No," I blurt. "That's the worst thing you could do right now. Stay away from her, Cassie."

"What's going on with her? You know, don't you?"

"It's nothing, Cass. Please, it's just a rough patch. Can you give us some space right now to sort things out?"

"You'll be careful?"

"Don't worry about me. I'll be fine."

She takes a seat on the bed next to me and leans her head on my shoulder. "I can't lose you too, Johnny. Please don't follow her down the rabbit hole. Stay here with me."

———

My braining is spinning from what Cass just told me, not to mention from this entire fucked-up mess. I can't settle down. I feel like I'm going to crack any minute.

Love you, Becca texts me once I finally make it to bed. That's when I really do lose it. I run to the bathroom and throw up.

Ditto, I type after I get back to my room. *And by the way, your love makes me sick.* I decide to leave that last part out.

At this point, I know better than to make her mad. She's

on the verge of coming undone and I want to be out of the way when it happens.

All night I toss and turn, worried about her plans to visit Ethan in the morning. That hers will be the first face he sees in twelve hours. And if she's in the same condition she was tonight, he'll be terrified. I can't let that happen. This time, *I* have to make a move.

I get up early and take Dad's truck. I try to forget that I haven't driven anything in a year. The driver's seat feels foreign. The keys are heavy in my hand. I put the key into the ignition and turn, bringing the Tahoe to life. It roars with pride. I hold my breath and wait for a light to switch on in the house. It doesn't.

The truck putts in reverse, jerking down the driveway. I'm in full concentration mode, looking over my shoulder as I back up. I never would've looked over my shoulder in the past unless there were little kids playing in the yard—the rearview mirror was always enough to do the trick. The kids, though, they were regulars in our yard because Mom was always bringing out lemonade and cookies. She's rolling over in her grave now at what we've done to Ethan. What we've done … shit. I can't even think the words "kidnap" or "hostage."

I'm in a cold sweat as I head to the ruins, waiting for a car to jump out in front of me at any moment. Waiting to be jackknifed by a semi or blindsided by a bread truck. I spent too much time studying all the photos from the accident.

My heart races, pumping hard as hell. Like it's trying to break free from my chest.

I get four blocks from my house and I can hardly breathe.
I have no choice but to turn around and head back home.

I'm such a pussy.

———————

On my morning ride with Cassie and Ava, I text the other
Johnny about the ammo. I have no idea how this is going to
all play out and I need the insurance. He says he can hook
me up during the lunch hour.

My backpack, which now houses the gun, sits next to me
in the backseat. I'll have to plant it outside by the Dumpsters
before I go into school, because there's no way I'm getting
past the metal detectors. So I lose the girls and take care of it.

By second period, I'm a complete head case. A few people
ask if I'm hungover. If only I was that lucky. When Travis Kent
walks into class, he doesn't look any better. Crescents of purple
and blue hang under his eyes. He has the same shirt on as yesterday, all soft and rumpled.

When I get to class, he's already sitting there with an
eerie, blank look on his face.

I take my seat and Mrs. Skye begins talking about divi-
sion of land and some other bullshit. Travis doesn't settle in.
I can hear him behind me fidgeting. Fingernails, pencils,
the palm of his hand, strumming and tapping on the desk.
The rustle of his sweatpants as he shifts around in his seat.
God, how I wish one damn thing could be normal today. I
wish he'd fall asleep and never wake up.

Travis has a backpack with him. Unusual. It's like he's

planning to go somewhere after class. The black bag is covered in gamer stickers and sits between our desks on my right side. The zipper is broken, split along the top, and the teeth are struggling to keep their grip. Inside the bag, I can see a gray T-shirt, water bottles, and tiny bags of chips.

It's obvious he received Becca's message about Ethan. But what I don't know is what he plans on doing about it. What exactly did Becca tell him? What's up her sleeve this time? I haven't talked to her since we left the library last night, but I'm sure she hasn't stopped working.

Where does she want to take Travis tonight?

How do we know he won't (or hasn't) called the police yet?

The questions ping around in my mind, and I have to bite my lip to stay silent.

Welcome to Hush

Responsible:
    We were fighting.
    We'd been fighting a lot more lately. Something changed, and I felt a wedge growing between us.
    I didn't like it.
    That night, it all came to a head.
    I could feel the tension building all day.
    And then … it ended in one big explosion.

25

JOHNNY

Becca and I don't say much throughout the following day at school. Though I watch everyone's comings and goings, from class to class. If they only knew how lucky they are.

The guilt, the guilt is what's going to kill me. Though it was like this even before the plan. Before I agreed. At that time, I'd fallen so hard for Becca I couldn't see my way out.

"Guilt is not a useful emotion, Johnny," Becca would say. "It's not productive and it only hurts you. At least change it to anger or something. Anger is a great motivator. Anger is the catalyst for getting things done."

Now I just have twice the guilt.

When Becca first started tutoring me, I was so far behind in every single class. Especially in Lit. We spent the spring reading Shakespeare and Hemingway and the Brontë sisters.

So different, yet so much the same.

Love, revenge, hate, jealousy...anger. The stories are always about the same thing.

If I were a chick, I'd tell you it was the best spring of my life. My world cracked wide open, and I felt my broken heart finally starting to heal.

And at the center of everything was Broken Girl.

The best part? I was starting to heal her too.

She'd wait for me after baseball practice, and even talked to the coach about my tutoring and got me playing in the games again. She quickly became my everything.

I try not to think about it and instead focus on Ethan, locked away. I have to find a way to help him. I have to.

When we finally make it to the end of the day, there's a note in my locker:

Do I still fit with you, Johnny?

It tears me up. How am I now the one who's afraid of my feelings? How did we change places? More importantly, how could I still have feelings for this psycho?

I take the note, put it in my chest pocket, send Cassie a text telling her I have a ride, and jog out to the parking lot to catch Bec.

She's leaning up against her car, staring out across the street and chewing on the inside of her cheek when I spot her.

I break into a sprint.

When she turns, her lips turn up and I swear there's a tear in her eyes. I shove my hands in my pockets because she's like a wild animal and I don't want to scare her away.

I move slowly, extending my hand to her.

She instantly grabs it and my entire body is a live wire of nerve endings. A buzz runs from head to toe and I squeeze her hand back. I'm disgusted by the effect she has on me. I also know I have no control over it.

"Where to?" I ask.

"My place," she whispers.

We hold hands the entire way home.

––––––––––

Becca leads me into her room. It feels like it might be the last time. I need the connection to her. I actually need it. I can't do another thing without it. It's physical and mental and spiritual, my feelings for this girl. It's all consuming and I feel like I can't breathe without her.

She sits on the bed and reaches out to me.

I don't go to her right away. In my mind, I know I need to protect myself. But the craving I have for her is stronger. I try to fight it, but when I look at her, I'm entranced and I want to let go of everything. I want to forget.

Becca's hair is wild before she smoothes it over to the side so it hangs over her shoulder. Her lips shine after licking them in anticipation of my kiss. Her long, ivory arms welcome me. But what gets me the most is the way her green eyes grow dark.

I move slowly to the bed and she scoots toward the wall to make room for me.

"I want you," she says. "Badly."

Her words shoot right to my groin. And as much as I want to run, my body has other ideas.

26

....

BECCA

....

As Johnny and I grew closer, we began to change. Johnny's insecurities morphed into confidence, and the heaviness he always carried around seemed to lighten. I felt lighter too. And I started to embrace the excitement he offered. Though Johnny's version of excitement wasn't dark or dangerous like Travis's brand of fun.

One day, Johnny even talked me into going to a party.

"So, Waters, what kind of craziness do you have planned for the weekend?" he asked during one of our tutoring sessions at the coffee shop a few block from my house.

"Study group on Saturday," I told him, not looking up from my book. He was supposed to be reviewing his math lesson so I could quiz him at the end of our session, but it was difficult to keep him on task.

"Oh, impressive," he said, taking a swig of his Coke. "You actually have plans. With people?"

"Mmmhmm, it's going to be outrageous," I said, trying to

mimic the voice my sister always used when talking to boys. For once I didn't attempt to hide my smile.

He looked at the title of my book and read it aloud— "*Gödel, Escher, Bach: An Eternal Golden Braid*"—with a raised brow. "And the rest of the time you're going to be reading this, aren't you?"

"*GEB* happens to be a beloved book of my people," I told him, sipping my tea.

"I have a better idea," he said, closing my book and pulling it out of reach. "Come with me to a party."

"A party?" *He wanted to take* me *to a party?*

"Yes," he answered, drawing out the word.

Silence.

"A party," he continued. "People, drinks, food, fun? Ring a bell?"

"Not particularly," I said, trying to make a grab for the *GEB* before he slapped my hand.

"There may even be some dancing. I heard a band is setting up in the garage."

"I don't see how that's a selling point for you, Johnny." I grimaced. "I don't dance."

"I bet you can and you just don't know it." He stood up from the booth and began to move. "Plus, I'm a great teacher. Look at my hips, for Christ's sake. You won't go wrong with me."

"I didn't say I *can't* dance." I watched his moves with increased interest. "I said I *don't* dance."

"Why?" He pulled me out of the booth then and spun me around. "I'm sure you dance just fine."

"No, I'm an incredible dancer. As you say—look at *my* hips."

He wasn't shy when he did.

"I have a better idea," I told him, stopping him as he was about to dip me.

"Let's hear it." He returned to his seat and I followed.

"I'll go to the … what are they calling it? Rendezvous in the Relics."

"Whoa, wait a minute. You know about those? I'm impressed."

"You're forgetting who my sister is—was," I said, regretting the words as they left my mouth.

"I never forget that, Becca," Johnny said. "Never." Then he squeezed my hand to lighten the mood. "So, go on. If you go to the Rendezvous … "

"Then you will read *GEB*," I said, sure this would deter him.

"Done," he said as soon as the words left my mouth. "Spending a weekend reading in exchange for a date with you? And your dancing hips? It's a no-brainer."

So there we were a few days later at the Rendezvous in the Relics, deep in the Detroit ruins. Brit would've lost her mind if she saw me. I'd heard there was a party every weekend, but they regularly changed location so the police—or, to be more precise, the criminals—didn't catch on. The police had bigger fish to fry. And with more 80,000 abandoned buildings to consider, the choices were endless.

That got me thinking about something else entirely.

But when Johnny and I arrived, I was completely out of

my comfort zone. I gnawed at my nails, biting them down to the quick. The people, the noise, the activity—it was sensory overload.

Johnny took my hand and introduced me to a few people and actually let me talk. He was completely relaxed, not like when Brit brought me places. She was always on edge and had a habit of answering for me.

We split a beer and talked most of the night.

Everything with Johnny was easy.

He pulled me onto the makeshift dance floor and he wasn't kidding about his hips. Then we got separated in the crowd.

It was just for a minute or two, but that's all it took.

A low voice hissed in my ear.

Travis.

"I see you, Bec," he said. "I always see you."

27

Becca, I want you to tell me something," I say as we lie in her bed. It's the only time she seems to be in the moment with me and lets down her guard.

"Okay," she mumbles, rolling onto her side, and it's so sexy I almost don't want to ask. I want to go for round two instead.

"When did you first decide to take Ethan?" I ask, toying with a lock of her hair to distract her. "Did you plan it the entire time?"

"I had everything planned out the entire time," she says without wavering.

It's not the answer I was hoping for.

I let her words roll around in my head for a while until it all begins to make sense. The way we met. How perfect it was. The timing. The mood. The circumstances. I question if *I* was part of the plan from the very beginning.

"Me too?" I ask, wanting to get to the truth. "Was I part of your plan?"

"Of course," she says, and I let her hair slide from my fingers.

"What do you mean, of course?" I try to keep the hurt from my voice.

"Well, that's how it started. I thought we'd make a good team. But this?" she says, pointing to the two of us in bed. "This is something I couldn't have ever predicted."

I'm not sure if that's a good or bad thing. But the fact that she thinks it's no big deal that she befriended me for this plan? That she tricked me? She doesn't get it. She honestly doesn't get it, and I don't think I'll ever be able to explain it to her.

"Did you pick me because I'm an easy target?" I continue to push, sitting up now. "Easy to control?" I ask.

Because I'm stupid?

"No, I picked you because he hurt both of us," Becca says. "I knew you were in as much pain as I was. The only thing good that's come of this." She runs her hand down my arm. "Us. I'm not ashamed of reaching out to you. It was the best thing I ever did. The smartest move I've ever made."

Again, she's so confident, so sure. It's hard not to believe her.

"You don't get it, Johnny." She puts a hand to my chest, and it's both comforting and irritating. "You have all the power now. You know all my secrets. I'm here, in this crazy situation, for you."

And then she kisses me.

———

Becca is making us sandwiches downstairs in the kitchen when her parents get home. Mr. and Mrs. Waters are *The Walking Dead.* Each evening, they shuffle in. They grunt and groan, occasionally throwing in a one-syllable word.

I think Cass has it wrong. I think Becca's parents want to send her away because they can't be bothered to take care of themselves, let alone their messed-up daughter. I think she's become a painful, living reminder of all they've lost.

Mrs. Waters wears an ugly brown cardigan. She has it gathered in the middle, secured with one button. Except it's in the wrong hole. She works at a bank, and Mr. Waters works at the courthouse. He's just as unkempt as the missus, with coffee stains that trickle down the length of his shirt.

I welcome them home. "Hi, Mr. and Mrs. Waters."

"Johnny," Mr. Waters grunts as he throws the keys in a dish on the table.

Mrs. Waters brushes past me to pat Becca on the head. Her hand strokes, bats, and misses, like a blind woman trying to locate her seeing eye dog.

Pat.

Pat.

Her pinkie finger pokes Becca in the eye.

Becca doesn't acknowledge her parents.

"Come on, Johnny," she says. "Eat up. We need to get going."

We move out to the front stoop and stuff our mouths with PB and Js. I eat two to Becca's one. We need our strength; there's another long night ahead.

The Elements of a Crime:
The Burden of Proof and
Presumption of Innocence

The burden of proof and the presumption of innocence are truly the foundation of criminal law. It is the most basic rule: the accused is presumed innocent until proven guilty. Music to the ears of criminals around the world. Can I get an *Amen*?

Just as important: the burden of proof lies with the prosecution. And one of the key elements in criminal liability is that the crime must be proven beyond reasonable doubt.

For lesser crimes (like robbery, for example), the elements of action and intention might be enough to win a case. But for the more serious crimes (like homicide), *all* elements of criminal liability must be proven.

In these crimes, one legal requirement is the rule of *corpus delicti*, which actually means "body of the crime." It means that to convict someone of murder, there must be a body.

This is where I should've been more careful.

28

At the party, Johnny introduced me to his sister, Cassie—an alternative girl who Brit would've called an unfortunate waste of good genes. Brit hated odd-colored hair, and ink, and piercings. Yes, she favored pretty and pastels. My poor simple sister thought she was Country Club material. Truth was, we were all trash, and only a few of us were going to get out. My sister wouldn't be one of them, and I could predict Johnny's sister wouldn't make it either.

But that didn't mean she wasn't valuable. She was. And I worked her from that very first moment. She took me in immediately. It was strange—the weaker I appeared, the stronger, and more protective, her feelings grew. She treated me like a fragile bird that could break at any moment. She assumed I was innocent; assumed I was good for her brother.

"You've helped bring him back to life," she told me once. She was so loyal to him. Just as he was to her. It hurt to be around them, because it reminded me what I never had with my sister.

I endured it because I needed Cass. She was useful and she'd help keep Johnny in line. I wasn't foolish enough to believe I could control him on my own. Not with what was coming.

29

L et's go." Becca makes her way to the car. I'm two steps behind her.

"Got the gun?" she asks.

"Yeah," I say, holding up my backpack, which I dug out of the trash at last bell. In addition to the gun, my bag is full of new supplies—including the bullets. I walked over to the gas station during lunch to meet the other Johnny and get the ammo, and also picked up some more food and water. Going to the station is something I do often—I always need something to eat and a power drink during baseball and in the workout season—so nothing looked suspicious. I've been taught well.

Becca slides into the driver's seat, but I catch the door before she closes it.

"Let me put this in the trunk," I say before reaching past her to pop the lever.

I hear her loud exhale as I head to the back of the car. The very next moment, she's at my side. It's unnerving.

Once I lift the hood to the trunk—and get a look at what's inside—I know why.

My brain goes haywire as I try to think of the word.

The word that matches what I see lying in the back of the trunk.

I try to grab on to it, but I can't.

It's too slippery.

30

After the Rendezvous in the Relics, I heard from Travis more regularly. But he was smart. He always made sure to cover his tracks. Still, I knew it was him—the calls, the notes, the way he watched me. He was angry and he was fixating again.

Just like he did with Brit.

"Why does she hate me so much?" he used to ask me, over and over again. "Why can she just leave us alone?"

He started keeping tabs on her—her friends and the guys she dated. And he'd dig up dirt on them, to prove that the people she associated with were no better than he was.

Brit became the topic of choice.

"Did you know Brit got a D in Chemistry? I heard she was smoking, drinking, messing around…" He'd fire out these accusations whenever we were together.

Travis was completely obsessed with her.

I felt those same eyes, and that same scrutiny, coming down on me as the months passed. I had to work fast. Thankfully, that party in the ruins gave me an idea.

Soon, *I* became just as consumed, developing a laser focus as my plan started to take shape.

Little by little, I brought Johnny in. I told him about Brit. About Travis's threats. About Brit being at Travis's before the accident.

Johnny grew more and more irate with each new revelation. Though I never told him it was really me who'd dated Travis. No, no, no. That would've messed up everything. I needed to play to his emotions. Play the part of the innocent. The victim.

I told Johnny it was Brit who planned to break up with Travis—I didn't think he'd trust me otherwise. I had to protect myself and keep Johnny close. I knew just how to do that—after all, I'd learned from the best. And as much as it pained me to use and manipulate people like Travis did, I had to. It was the only way it was going to work.

Welcome to Hush

Responsible:

Why are some murders described as grisly and heinous? Is there really such a thing as a nice murder?

Aren't they all grisly and heinous?

In my case, I'd say the scene was most defi-nitely heinous. The death was simply necessary. Some might even say it was deserved. I know one person who would say that.

The second victim, though? Well, that was just unfortunate.

31

······················

JOHNNY

······················

Do you believe in God?" I asked Becca one night after we'd messed around in her bedroom. She was always talkative after, and it was the only time I had access to the unsolvable puzzle that was her mind.

"God?" she asked, straightening her bed.

"Yeah," I said, zipping my pants. "The Big Guy Upstairs. The Higher Power. Father Almighty. You know, God."

"Noooo," she sang, like it was a trick question or something. "Nor does any respectable scholar."

"You don't ever feel anything from Brit?" I asked. "A feeling or a sign?

"Are you for real? You don't have an Ouija board in that backpack, do you?"

"Hey, I'm being serious here. You get to blather on to me day in and day out about literature and science and math—"

"Which I'm doing to help you get a proper college scholarship," she interrupted.

"Yes, and which I'm totally grateful for—especially when

you wear these sexy glasses." I snatched them off her face. She held out her palm—no fun.

"I just mean, we talk about things all day, but sometimes I feel like I don't really know you."

"So, you go right for the Big Guy?" She smiled then. "That's pretty deep."

"Yeah, it's just, sometimes, I don't know. I think I feel my mom, and I was wondering if you ever feel Brit."

"Oh that?" Becca pursed her lips like she did when she was ready to go into full-on lecture mode. "Yes, I do feel Brit, and I believe you feel your mom. But it's not really them. It's their energy. That kind of thing has been documented."

"Do you always have to be such know-it-all, Waters?" I asked.

"No." She smiled. "Not always. This shirt is Brit's, actually. I feel her energy when I wear it."

God, where did *that* girl go? I miss her so much.

Ever since we started this stupid plan, I've seen less and less of the person I thought I knew. The only thing we've talked about for months is Travis Kent. The only thing I see in her eyes now is pain and anger.

It scares the shit out of me.

32

BECCA, THE ANNIVERSARY

Revenge had become my religion.

It was really—finally—happening. Johnny was on edge, but I was excited and ready to go. I couldn't wait. I felt alive for the first time since, well, the last time. The last plan I'd had with Travis, to get Brit off our backs.

"Brit is coming to see you tomorrow," I'd told him when we snuck off to our favorite dark corridor in the school basement the day before the accident.

"Let me guess—another lecture about how you're so fragile and why I have to stop seeing you?" He'd sounded bored, but his fingers kept busy finding their way under my shirt.

I knew Brit said things like that about me, but to actually hear it made my blood boil. It also made me feel justified in what I was about to do.

"No," I told him, melting into his touch. Brit was out of her mind; Travis Kent was very, very good for me. "She's coming as me."

"Explain." He removed his hands and met my eyes.

I had his attention.

"She discovered that we're still together and she made a few threats."

"And?" he asked, gritting his teeth in that way of his.

"She told me to break up with you, but I refused."

"I'd hope so." He chuckled.

"Then she said that if I didn't break up with you, she would. It's that or she tells my parents. So she's coming to see you—pretending to be me—to end it once and for all."

"Is she now?" Travis took my hand and pulled me to him. "Well, what do you say we end this little routine once and for all?"

I answered with a kiss, thinking we had it under control.

That was my ultimate mistake. I underestimated him.

I should've taken his threat seriously, but that was back when I was using my heart rather than my head. I believed he was just going to scare her. Play some kind of trick or mind game. He was good at that sort of thing.

That's what I wanted to believe. If I'd been using my brain, I would've seen the signs. I could've predicted the outcome. But all I could think about at the time was how nice it'd be to watch *her* squirm for a change.

Stupid.

People can really mess up some of the best-laid plans. The human factor is the most difficult challenge to overcome, because people are unpredictable.

You can have everything mapped out down to the most minute detail, and someone will do something completely unexpected. That's why I prefer to spend my time working with numbers rather than working with people. You always know what you can expect with numbers.

With Travis, I knew he was volatile, unpredictable, dangerous. I also knew Brit wouldn't back off even if he threatened her. Still, I wouldn't give him up. See? Completely out of character for someone like me.

So I'd gone ahead and told him her plan. I set her up. Of course, I did it to gain back some control. To get Brit off my case and to get my own identity back. I couldn't handle being under her thumb for one moment longer.

What didn't I expect? For Travis to become so deranged that he'd smack Brit around, chase her off his property, and follow her in his truck, eventually running her off the road.

Unpredictability in all its glory.

Travis wasn't even sorry about Brit. He never once showed remorse or uttered any type of apology. He never mentioned it. Out of sight, out of mind. I hated him for that. But I hated myself more.

Now my sister was dead.

For that short time with Travis, I was distracted, and I ended up paying the ultimate price. Now all I could feel was the empty space that Brit had once filled. I still ached for my life before the accident, when there wasn't the enormous imbalance. But that ache also fueled me, and I let the fire rage. And that's when I knew that his confession wouldn't be enough. I wanted more, and I knew how we could make Travis pay.

Take the only person he ever really cared about and even the score.

Travis had no mother figure in his life, which explained a lot. What he did have was a distant father and several bitchy ex-girlfriends. That was his life. But there was one person who mattered. Someone he cared for a great deal. His brother.

33

....

JOHNNY

....

"Ah, ah, ah." The sound rattles in my brain, though I could also be talking aloud. I'm not sure. Everything is swimmy. Underwaterish. Foggy.

I shake my head, but the image doesn't go away. I want to be done with all of this right now. I want to run, but it feels like my legs are buried in the ground; I can't move them.

Turning to Becca, I see her mouth moving. I don't register anything she says until somehow, I'm able to pull the plug in my head and the water slowly goes down the drain. Things begin to clear and I can hear Becca's voice.

"Wait," she says.

I ignore her command, though, because I found the word.

The word that matches what I see.

There, in Becca's trunk, is a tool. A large, flat spade. A shovel.

A shovel that wasn't there yesterday.

It's resting on another piece of plastic—the same kind we used for Ethan—and it's covered in clumps of black dirt. It may as well be a body.

34

I gathered everything I would need for the night. Plus a few extras to keep Johnny under control. He wasn't going to be happy with the way things were about to go down. But if he didn't play nice, I had the drugs.

And if it came down to it, I could always use Cass.

I wouldn't like it, but I'd do it.

Last time I made mistakes, I let my feelings for Travis get in the way. This time I would think with my head. To hell with my heart.

This time, things would end on my terms.

35

....

JOHNNY

....

The clumps of dirt on the tip of the spade tell me the tool has been used recently. The duct tape around the middle tells me it came from our garage.

I broke the handle when I was digging up part of our yard for Mom's garden. It was the spring before the accident, and the ground was still cold and hard. I taped it up so I wouldn't get a splinter. The garden was our Mother's Day gift to Mom. I did the heavy labor and Cass bought all the seeds and starter plants. She also worked on the design.

When we were done, we took Mom out with a blindfold on, making a big production out of our gift. When she took it off and saw the tilled dirt and seedlings and rows of markers of her favorite vegetables, she cried.

It was a good day.

That summer we had peppers and tomatoes and onions. Our entire neighborhood was stocked in homemade salsa. Mom would be out there for hours in a funny-looking floppy hat—pruning, watering, and talking to her plants.

It hurts to think about her.

And now our shovel is tainted and my memory is dirty. I hate Becca for that. But I guess it all makes absolutely perfect sense.

Why would Becca use her own shovel to bury a body?

Why risk it, when her idiot boyfriend could just as easily take the fall?

I can see it in police evidence now. Sprinkled in white powder so they can gather the fingerprints. My fingerprints. Who else would they belong to?

"Where did you bury him?" one of the officers would scream. He's the bad cop.

The other, older man in uniform would say, "We know you had a good reason. I'm sure he had what was coming to him. But son, you need to tell us where you buried him." He's the good cop.

"I don't know what you're talking about," I'd tell them. "I didn't bury anyone. I didn't hurt anyone."

My insides flicker when I say it.

Even in my imagination, I know it's a lie.

I take the gun from my backpack and slide it into the waistband of my jeans.

———

Becca looks around to be sure nobody else has seen what I just did. She slams the trunk shut and rushes into the car.

I open the driver's side door and force her to move over

into the passenger seat. Then I hit the safety locks, and this time I have no trouble driving to the site.

Once we get there, I grip Becca's arm, pull her from the car, and drag her down the hill.

"Hang on." She fights me the entire way down. "Will you just listen to me?"

"Not another fucking word, Becca." I don't stop moving. Not. Another. Word.

"It's not what you think," Becca tells me as we get closer to the decrepit library.

Her words are drowned out by the creepy music playing in my head. The kind that indicates trouble ahead. With each step we take down the hill, it gets louder. Faster. Harder.

My heart pounds to the beat that echoes in my mind. My legs fight through the tall grass and weeds. My head prepares for what I might find in that room as one singular thought consumes me.

Ethan.

Once we're on level footing, I run to the building. Becca's on my heels.

Her hand grabs my arm when we reach the door. She's fast.

"Listen." She fights to catch her breath. "The shovel was for the clothes, Johnny. I buried his soiled clothes."

I can hear her above the music now, but I don't believe her. Every fiber of my being tells me there's danger. Serious danger.

I look in the peep hole, but I don't see him. The bed is empty. It's what I was afraid of. Ethan's gone.

Becca took care of him.

I drop my head and Becca looks at me, confused. "What?" she asks. "What is it?"

"Where did you put him, Becca?" It's hard to get the words out.

"What do you mean? He's here. He's here, right?"

She storms into the room. She stands over the empty bed.

"This isn't right," she says. Her eyes scan every inch of the space. "No, this can't be right."

Then there's a horrible coughing, gagging-like sound.

"Ethan?" Becca finally uses his name. "Johnny, come here. He's on the floor."

I rush over to her, on the side of the bed, and there's Ethan, sandwiched between the metal bedframe and the wall. I want to be relieved, but the bright yellow vomit and bile covering his sweatshirt scream that he's anything but okay.

"I think he's having a reaction to the drugs." Becca's back to her calm, icy demeanor.

"We need to get him to the hospital." I say.

"No, we don't." She digs in.

"Are you crazy? Seriously? You want him to die here?"

I really think she might.

"I know how to handle this," she says. "He threw up— that's a good thing. I know you're freaking out. I don't blame you, I blame him. He's hurt you, Johnny. Worse than I thought. I'm sorry about that. I'm sorry about it all. I won't shut you out anymore. And when there are hard decisions to be made, we'll make them together. I promise."

It takes me a second to catch it. But she's just let me know that there'll be more hard decisions to come. I don't even want to know how difficult they're going to be.

We clean Ethan up. Change his shirt (Becca has a change of clothes ready—she went to Target to get supplies when I went to the gas station). We give him water and settle him in bed, and soon he drifts off to sleep.

It takes a long time.

When we're done, I walk halfway up the hill and sit. I stare at the sky until the sun goes down. The darkness sets in—outside, inside. It's cold and empty and evil.

Becca doesn't join me. I'm sure she's doing more scheming down in the building. I'm happy for the space; I can't be around her right now.

"Time to get your opponent," she says, finally showing herself. She doesn't stop as she walks up the hill toward her car.

Oh, he's my opponent now?

If I didn't know better, I'd say my girl is fucking with me.

Mind games. It's what she's good at. Pull you in, push you away. Offers her body, but keeps her heart closed off. Builds you up, only to tear you down. She knows exactly what she's doing.

That's when I know, I'm stuck. She planned everything from the very beginning—maybe even including a way out if things go to shit. There's no question that I'll be on the losing side if that happens. There are too many things linking me to this crime.

I have to come up with a back-up plan of my own.

36

....

BECCA

....

After I tricked Johnny into taking Ethan, the real competition was finally underway. Of course, the entire year was nothing but sport. Tricks and manipulations. A game of strategy where you attack and capture.

There were so many moves—and countermoves—that I knew Johnny was having a hard time distinguishing fact from fiction. That's just how it was supposed to be. I wove quite the complex web.

I discovered who killed your mom and Brit. Overstatement. My sister had already told me, right before she was crushed to death.

I've never had a real boyfriend. Exception: Travis. The murderer.

We're in this together. But I was running the show.

We won't hurt him. Lie. That was precisely what we were going to do.

I love you. Verdict was still out.

Then there were all the omissions. I mean, I wasn't technically lying, those first few days when Johnny asked how I was coping. I simply didn't need to tell him I'd been on lockdown after Brit died. I didn't need to tell him about the psychiatrist. That was nobody's business. I told him about the support group, and that was enough. If he'd known much more, there's no way he would have trusted me. He'd act just like Brit or my parent or my teachers. He would have looked at me like *I* was the crazy one.

I couldn't have him look at me that way.

And this was my last chance. Unfortunately, I'd just learned that morning it was back to lock-up for me. But not the cushy old fourth floor. No, my parents wanted to send me to some "center" to get my head right.

You're not right, they kept telling me. *You're just not right.*

It had been arranged. I would leave in two days.

And that meant I had nothing to lose.

37

JOHNNY

We drive to the other end of town, passing the bodega along the way. I hear Poppy's voice in my head: *Any sign of trouble, primo, you come to me.*

If he only knew.

As Becca drives, I continue to work out the details of my back-up plan. Thankfully, I've always worn gloves at the ruins. Always. I know there are things that will still link me to Ethan, but nothing I can't handle. Nothing I can't take care of.

My mind begins to form a list. My *Get Out of this Clusterfuck* list. It's a short one.

- Shovel
- Gun
- Girl

Actually, I may need to change the order.

- Shovel

- Girl

- Gun

Take care of those three things and then I'm out. I'm done. I just need to tick them off, one at a time. To do that, I need to follow Becca a little while longer. I also have to be sure. If I use my back-up plan, it'll destroy everything Becca and I have together. There's no way she'll trust me again. Can I live with that? Can I live without her? I'm afraid I'll never be able to answer that question.

Once we get to the accident scene, we park in the abandoned parking lot and Becca tells me to keep a lookout.

"I'm going to get Travis," she says.

"Alone?" I ask.

She nods. "Meet me in the ditch by the road, in exactly seven minutes."

I'm not going to argue. I have work to do, and just as soon as she's out of the car, I get to it.

Shovel.

One side of the lot borders the woods. I quickly pop the trunk, grab the shovel, and head into the tree cover as deep as I can. Scanning the area, I spot an old log.

I check my phone.

Four minutes left.

I roll the log over and dig.

Three minutes.

Placing the shovel in the hole, I roll the log back over it. I'll have to come back later because I can't have this thing biting me in the ass down the road, but this should hold me for now.

One minute, thirty seconds.

I sprint to get to Becca in time.

When I do, she has Travis flat on his back in the ditch. The syringe is still stuck in his neck.

"He went down fighting," she says.

"I can see that," I say, looking at his body contorted into a pretzel. "So what does that Beautiful Mind have planned now? This location isn't exactly private, Bec."

"Call me romantic," she says, the ice back in her voice. "I thought it seemed appropriate."

"I appreciate it, I do. But how did he get here?"

"Cab," she answers.

Always an answer.

"I take it he now knows we're behind the kidnapping?"

"He's getting the idea." She smiles. "Let's take him to his brother."

"Okay," I tell her. "This is your show."

She seems pleased with that response.

I wait with Travis while Becca retrieves the car and pulls over at the side of the road. I quickly get Travis inside, though the sound of him hitting the sterile plastic in the backseat has my gagging reflex going again.

I try not to think of it and instead focus on the next two items on my list: Girl and Gun.

Once we get back to the ruins, the sky is black. No stars; no moon. A new chill in the air has me zipping up my coat.

Haunted by the twisted déjà vu, I scoop up Travis and follow Becca to the library.

I drop him on the bed next to his brother, who happens to be in a very deep sleep, and lock his arms and legs in the restraints.

Then Becca and I wait.

The Elements of a Crime:
#4 Causation

In some crimes, like murder or assault, actual harm must occur. In homicide, there must be a killing. For assault, there must be bodily injury. Without the harm—causation—the crime would not exist.

Causation can be hard to prove because there could be intervening events that occurred in between the act and the result. So the act and the result must be close together in time. Or it must be proven that the guilty party set a chain of events in motion that eventually led to a harmful result.

In my case, the proximity of the crime and harmful result are pretty damn close.

That's if the right person knows where to look.

I'm worried that Johnny and Becca know where to look.

That's why I went on Hush to confess. Becca hacked my computer, like I knew she would, and I had to throw her off Ethan's scent. It's always been about keeping my brother safe.

If it was just me implicated, I'd have more options. I could run; I could go after Becca. I could let the cops take me—it's not like my life hasn't been destroyed anyway. But it's not just me. I have Ethan to think about. I'm responsible for him. If I don't look out for him, who will?

Ethan's just a kid, doing what kids do. He was trying to earn my respect when he went after Brit.

Truthfully, I think the bitch got what she deserved.

38

My mind drifts as we wait for the Kent boys to wake up, and the story of Becca and Johnny plays in my head. Maybe because I know it's coming to an end. I know that after tonight, there will be no more Becca and Johnny.

I know it's twisted, but I'm not happy about that. Not one bit.

Becca invaded my life when I needed her. Made me laugh and cry and want to be better. She made me stand up for myself. She made me feel like a man.

Big time.

"Don't you dare slut shame her, Johnny Vega," Cassie said when I told her about my first time with Becca.

I'd drifted away from most of my guy friends at that point, but I had to tell somebody about Becca and her, uh, appetite. I mean, I was in that comfortable sweet spot between the players and the sad saps who wouldn't see a vagina until college. I was perfectly content that I could count the number sexual experiences I'd had with girls on two hands. Those who I'd sealed the deal with could be counted on one. Absolutely acceptable.

But never—never—had I experienced anything like Becca.

So I told Cassie, and even she was impressed.

We'd been dating for four months at that point, and I planned a special night to celebrate. After our dinner and movie, things got a little heated in the car. Shirts were off and hands were exploring and soon we were reaching the point of no return. But I didn't want it to be like this—in the car, after talking about my mom. I couldn't switch on and off like Becca could. I couldn't be logical about this.

"Slow down," I whispered to her.

"Why?" she asked.

When it happened, I wanted to be in bed. I wanted to take my time; I wanted to spend the night with her. I'm sure that sounds like a pathetic chick flick, but I wanted it to be special. I wanted to bring my A game. But I couldn't tell her this. She'd probably laugh me out of the car.

"I don't want to do it here," I told her.

Becca palmed me through my jeans—she wasn't going to make this easy for me.

"You feel ready," she said, tightening her grip. And a bolt of lightning struck me right there.

"I want this to be special for you," I told her.

"I'm with you, Johnny. Someone who makes me feel good. It's going to be special. I think it'll make us feel better too. Did you know people who have regular intercourse live five years longer and have fewer health problems?"

Who was this girl?

"Please never say the word 'intercourse' again." I shuddered. "It gives me the creeps."

She got a gleam in her eye. How I loved it when feisty Becca made a rare appearance.

"Intercourse," she said again. And again. And again.

Until I stopped her.

———————

Of course Becca got her way. Not that it was a sacrifice on my part. It was just unexpected. I held her after that for a long time. One of the only times she really let me in.

Yes, we did it. It was amazing, and I'll never be the same.

It's these memories that make me question everything I'm about to do. But as I look at the two brothers on the bed, with that same pudgy face, long nose, and thin lips, I realize I don't have a choice.

39

Travis contacted me shortly after I sent the fake message about his brother's kidnapping. As expected, he was desperate to save his brother. After spending those months together, I knew how much Ethan meant to him. He and Johnny were the same that way—dedicated to their siblings.

It wasn't fair, and I felt the disparity of that every day.

When we were dating, I spent a lot of energy trying to convince Travis to quit gambling, especially once he started using my math skills to cheat, and to rip people off. That's how I knew to use the pissed-off gamer as an excuse to get him where I needed him.

It really could've happened. Those guys get desperate for their money.

So I knew all the right buttons to push. And once I did, I knew Travis would come to me.

"Bec, I'm in deep shit," he said when he called.

"What's going on?" I acted concerned, which should've have been his first tip-off.

He brought me up to speed on his situation and I listened, applying all the gasps and sighs in the right places.

"I'll meet you at the accident site tomorrow. Let me work on a few things and I'll help."

Now, you'd think a normal person would've felt sick sending that photo to Travis. Little Ethan hurt and soiled, leaning up against the lamppost. I'm sure a normal person would have. But I wasn't normal anymore. I was an animal at that point. Fighting for survival.

I was consumed by revenge, retribution, justice. It was all I could focus on. Making things equal.

Do to Travis what he did to me.

I just wasn't sure where that left Johnny.

40

....

JOHNNY

....

Watching Travis wake up is about the most disturbing thing I've ever seen in my life. I watch him from my designated spot in the small room as his head shifts from side to side. His eyebrows begin lifting as his brain tells him it's time to open his eyes. My hands are clammy and my head goes light before I realize I'm holding my breath. When I release it, I almost call out to him. But then I remember: I can't break the rules. Yet.

Travis lets out a soft moan and his head begins to bob.

One.

Two.

Three.

Grunt. Groan.

Becca is enthralled, watching the spectacle. But for her it's more fascination than disgust.

Travis stretches his arms and the sinews and veins bulge from his lean limbs. Then he stretches his legs. His toes point up in a pair of gray sneakers.

He must be dreaming still, because his head starts to shake

in a violent rotation. He blows out a gust of air and his bangs flutter. Mom used to do the same thing after working in the garden. The thought makes me remember why we're here.

Travis continues to thrash until he opens his eyes.

"What…" He coughs. "What's going on?"

He whimpers, like truly whimpers, when he spots his brother. It's hard to watch even though I detest the guy. His eyes dart across the room: to Ethan, Becca, Ethan, me, Ethan. He's putting it all together.

He drops his head and clears his throat. "There's no gamer, is there?"

His bottom lip trembles.

Becca slowly shakes her head.

41

....

BECCA

....

Travis had the cab drop him off by the ditch, as we'd discussed. Good little puppet. Johnny waited in the parking lot a little way up the hill. I had to play this very carefully because emotions were running wild.

That's why I had the back-ups. New pawns I could use if I had to.

"Can you help me?" Travis asked when I made my way to him on the side of the road. His eyes were bloodshot and puffy; he'd been up for twenty-four hours. "I know I don't deserve it, but I need you so much right now."

"Yes, of course," I told him, stuffing my hand into my pocket.

He reached out to hug me, and I was hyper alert. He could've had his own plans; he could've known what was in my hand.

I was cautious as I moved in and gave him a one-armed squeeze.

"I so sorry, Trav." I kept my hand wrapped around the syringe and out of sight.

Then, when he turned his back, I stuck the needle deep into his neck.

Welcome to Hush

Responsible:

> *It's not that I hate women.*
>
> *That's not it at all.*
>
> *I just hate women who are bitches. Women who think they're better than me.*
>
> *Yes, Freud, my mother left when I was young.*
>
> *Yes, it's true that my old girlfriend got hurt because of my temper.*
>
> *And yes, I'd rather play video games where I have control than live in the real world. Except when I was with my new love. She wasn't like the others. She treated me like I was the special one.*
>
> *Until her sister threatened all that. The one girl who had put me back together after the others tore me apart. Damn right I wasn't going to taking it lying down. I threatened her, scared her away.*
>
> *I didn't set out to kill her, but in the heat of the moment, yeah, I think I wanted her dead.*

42

JOHNNY

Ethan hasn't woken up, and I have the nagging feeling it's been way too long. The gun in my waistband is making me itchy.

"Okay." Travis trembles, looking over Ethan. "I'm here. Now let him go."

"Why do you think you're making the rules?" Becca asks. "You're here because I made it so."

"He's sick," Travis screams. "He has asthma. Whatever you gave him could kill him, Becca. Please. I'm here. I'll do whatever you ask, just let him go."

Becca doesn't even react to the asthma comment. It's clear that this isn't new information to her—people like Becca don't miss something this big. This type of mistake doesn't happen by chance. She knew about the asthma, which means it was part of the plan.

Ethan is going to die.

So my plan—Shovel, Girl, Gun—has to change.

Ethan has now popped to the top of my list. I have to save him.

I'm the only person who can.

Welcome to Hush

Responsible:

"I know who you are, bitch," I told her when she started making all those demands.

It might have ended there if she'd just let it go.

But she couldn't drop it.

"What are you talking about?" she asked, trying to look all indignant like her sister.

"Your sister told me you were coming. She told me all about your little plan to break us up."

Betrayal flashed across her face.

She'd been betrayed by her own sister.

Man, how I loved it.

43

JOHNNY

I go over my list. What I need to do before I bail out of this shithole. I have to focus to make it work.

- Ethan
- Girl
- Gun

"Do you know why you're here?" Becca asks Travis, completely ignoring Ethan.

"No, no I don't," Travis says. His eyes dart back and forth from his brother to Becca.

- Ethan
- Girl
- Gun

"Becca, look at Ethan," Travis pleads. "He's in bad shape. He needs a doctor."

"Hmm," she says, playing with her gloved fingers. "Like my sister needed a doctor?"

Travis's face gets all pinched.

"Johnny knows." Becca grins. "And soon he's going to know a lot more."

What the fuck is going on now? I'm not sure how much more I can take.

"I know you have some crazy idea going through your head," Travis says, pulling on his restraints. "But I have no idea what you're talking about."

"That's what you're going to go with?" Becca asks, picking up her school bag. "You sure about that ... *Responsible?*"

Travis's face pales and he swallows. Once. Twice. Three times.

"Dude." He looks to me now—desperate to be heard.

I pace the room, growing more confused, irritated, and downright panicked.

"She's lost it," Travis says to me, avoiding Becca's glare. "That's how she is. Let me and my brother go and I swear I never saw you, man. You can just get up and go."

Becca pulls out a stack of papers and walks over to me.

"What's that?" I ask in spite of myself. I have to know more about this latest development. It's too late to walk away.

"This?" Becca says, holding up the papers. "What don't you tell us, Travis?"

Welcome to Hush

Responsible:

After our confrontation, she took off in her car.

I followed.

Yes, I was trying to run her off the road. She was panicked and driving erratic.

I liked that.

I liked making her squirm.

Who's in charge now, bitch?

It was a fun game. I'd increase my speed, come up alongside the car, and start edging her to the center line. The tiny rocks from the shoddy road were pinging off her fender.

We were approaching the hill and I was thinking, this is going to be fun.

Until another car was coming toward us.

Then I edged her one last time.

44

....

JOHNNY

....

I listen to Becca, trying to make sense of what she's saying. I know she's trying to tell me something—something important about the papers. But at the same time, I catch Ethan out of the corner of my eye.

That's when the kid moves. His nose twitches and his lips pucker, like he might be awake. Then nothing.

"This is Travis's confession on Hush," Becca says. "He admits to everything. Causing the accident. Leaving the scene."

"If you have all of this, why didn't you just go to the police?" I ask, furious that we could've avoided this fuck-up. "Why did we have to do all of this?"

"It's not that simple," she says, her fingers stroking the paper. "He didn't use his own computer to write this, so there's no address. The site is designed to keep users anonymous."

"You know what?" I say, ready to make my move. I can't wait any longer. I pull the gun from my waistband and point it at Becca. "It doesn't matter anymore. This is done. I'm done."

"Wait, wait," she says. "There's more, Johnny. So much more."

45

....

BECCA

....

Johnny was turning on me, I could see it. It had happened gradually, but at that point he was in full-fledge desertion mode. Ready to throw me to the enemy at any time.

Of course, I knew about Ethan's asthma, and the drugs did pose a problem for him. But it wasn't like he was making his way out of here anytime soon. That was kind of the whole point. I mean, how could you make a monster like Travis Kent pay? Simple. You take away the person closest to him—the only person he's ever really cared about. Like he took Brit from me. Like he took Johnny's mom.

I found Travis's confession on Hush months ago. I knew he'd have to brag about it to someone. It must've killed him to remain anonymous. It was all right there, but I couldn't share it with Johnny. Not yet. Information like that had to be revealed carefully. Finally, it was time.

Once Johnny found out, he wouldn't be able to stop himself. He was explosive, ready to blow at any minute.

All I had to do was light the match.

"Go ahead, Travis," I said. "Tell Johnny what these papers say. Tell him what you did to our families."

Travis didn't move a muscle.

"You tell him," I said, "or I will."

Welcome to Hush

Responsible:

The crash was quick and brutal.

Metal scraping, tires squealing, glass breaking.

Then nothing. Smoke and quiet.

I pulled my truck past the two cars on the side of the road. I got out and ran back. That part was instinct. So was the next, I guess.

First, I went to the girl. She didn't move. I was sure she was dead. I'd later find out she wasn't, but it took a while for that to happen.

Then I went and looked at the other car. The woman.

She was still alive.

"Help," she said in a gurgly voice. Blood coming up her throat and spilling out of the sides of her mouth.

That's when I should've called. I should've done something.

But I didn't.

I just stood there and stared at the woman.

"Tell my family," she gurgled again. "Tell them I love them."

She sat there, trapped in her seat, trying to regulate her breathing.

Fighting for her life.

I made a point to nod at her request … before getting into my car and driving away.

46

Johnny still had the gun pointed toward me, but I knew he wouldn't shoot. This was part of his escape plan. Well, I'm sorry, but that was not going to happen. Not after we'd come this far.

Travis hadn't made any move to tell us about Hush, so I read his confessional. I read about the way he deliberately drove Brit into a head-on crash and left Johnny's mom to die.

"He was there when she died," I said to Johnny. "He was there."

Then I waited for it to register.

47

He was there," Becca says again. "He could've saved her. Your mom didn't have to die."

"No," I yell. "No."

My brain is racing, so I start pacing to keep up. Things are getting slippery again. Everything is jumbled, coming into my head out of order. Yet everything is moving so fast I can't organize it.

Brit.

Dead . . . blood . . . gurgling . . . family.

Goodbye . . . Mom . . . love . . . left.

Truck. Gurgle. Blood.

Save. Save. Save.

"You do what you need to do," I hear Becca say softly. "Nobody would blame you if you took Ethan. If you paid Travis back. We deserve justice. We all deserve it."

"Stop," I say. "Just stop."

Ethan begins to fade from my thoughts as my back-up plan changes again. Saving him is no longer my top priority.

The gun in my hand changes course—moving from Becca toward Travis.

The war begins: rage verses devastation.

I can't bear to think of Mom's final minutes. I can't handle knowing she suffered; she knew she was going to die. She saw Travis walk away from her.

Rage begins to win this battle.

I can't think around it.

I move closer to the scumbag.

A muffled cry comes from Travis. From his filthy mouth. Teardrops fall down his face and all I can think about is ripping him apart. And showing him. Showing him why it mattered that he left the scene. Making him understand exactly what he did.

Becca closes in on me—her tiger-and-prey move. She rests both hands on my arms, stroking them. Speaking in an almost soothing voice. Full of emotion. Her eyes dancing.

"No," Becca says. "Not Travis. You need to make him suffer. Hurting him will only make things easier. Put him in pain like he put us in pain. Point the gun at Ethan. Please, Johnny. For me."

Too much noise.

"Shut up. Shut up. Shut up."

My finger shakes on the trigger.

"You can do it," Becca says. "Yes, it's a perfectly logical response. It is justified. It evens things out. I would understand. And I'll support you. Whatever you need."

"Okay then," I spit, feeling my body heat with rage. Murderous rage. I'm discovering there is such a thing. "It's settled."

I move the gun once again.

48

I wanted him to do it. I needed him to do it.

I just had to play the game a little longer.

Though Ethan was my pawn, he was Travis's king. We had captured the king.

Checkmate.

It wasn't enough. We had to finish this.

"Pull the trigger," I said. I said it over and over.

Over Johnny's screams and Travis's cries.

"Ethan is still out. He won't even see it coming," I said. "It'll be peaceful. Not at all like what Travis did to our families."

Pull. The. Trigger.

The Elements of a Crime: Crime and Punishment

For every crime, there must be a punishment. At least in any civilized society, am I right? In the U.S., justifications for punishment falls into two categories:

- **Retributive:** claims that punishment is justified because the criminal deserves it.

- **Utilitarian:** claims that punishment is useful. The useful purposes of punishment are: prevention, rehabilitation, and incapacitation.

Then there are the six theories of criminal justice based on the following goals:

- **Retribution:** Eye for an eye. Fan favorite.

- **General Deterrence:** Punish the offender in order to send a message to the general population. (Done all the time in school.)

- **Specific Deterrence:** Punish the offender so they will not do the same thing again.

- **Rehabilitation:** Incarcerate the offender to *treat*

them, so they won't do anything like this again. For *their* own good.

- **Restraint/Incapacitation:** Incarcerate dangerous offenders to get them off the street and separate them from society; prevent future harm by these people. For *our* own good.

- **Public Education:** Communicate what values are important to society by determining what we punish.

Can you hear me up here on this pedestal?

———————

Becca would say I was a good candidate for all of these. In the end, however, she didn't think legal punishment was enough. She had a better way to make me suffer.

I knew I deserved it.

I deserved to be punished for a lot of things.

But Ethan didn't.

He was just a kid who was always getting messed up in things. In the wrong place at the wrong damn time. I would take the fall for him. I'd do anything.

Becca, though, she wanted his blood on my hands. Like Brit's blood was on hers.

What she didn't know—what the two of them will never know—was that it was Ethan's idea to go after Brit.

After her little scene, Brit stormed off. Ethan heard the entire exchange and just looked at me in disbelief. People didn't talk to me that way, and despite the fact that Ethan had never even liked Becca (he never liked anyone who got too close to me), he didn't like people telling me what to do.

We made our own rules.

I'd taught him that.

"You can't let her go, Johnny," he said. "Not after what she tried to do."

"It's okay," I told him. "Everything's going to be okay."

Then I thought about my next move.

Turns out, I didn't have to.

Ethan had already made the decision for me. He followed her.

He wanted to teach her a lesson.

Becca and Johnny can't find out about that.

Ethan has a long line of offenses—most in my honor. The rumors about me? They're mostly true. But it was Ethan who got me into the messes. Like the time he beat up on my ex-girlfriend because she cheated on me. Ethan heard her confession when she came out to the house. He just went ape shit on her.

He was dangerous. Still, I couldn't fault him for it, so I covered for him. He's been screwed with his whole life. I've been his only protection, and I wasn't about to stop. I told him I'd handle it.

And I did.

Too bad I got to the scene of the accident too late.

Brit, she deserved what happened. But I didn't want anyone else to get hurt. I really wanted to help Johnny's mom, but

I couldn't risk staying or calling it in. Ethan could be taken from us.

I couldn't do that to him.

So we left.

49

I still have the gun to Ethan's head. I don't want to pull the trigger. But I want to destroy Travis. More than I've ever wanted to do anything in my life.

Two birds, one stone.

But it doesn't matter what *I* want.

"Don't do it, man," Travis begs. "Don't do it."

I put the gun back in my jeans and I grab my knife instead.

"No, no, no," Travis chants.

Becca's eyes flicker, but she says nothing.

I take my knife and stand over Ethan.

"Johnny," Becca says. "Do it."

Then Cassie's voice rings in my ear: *Don't follow her down the rabbit hole.*

Travis cries.

It's just too much, so I grip my knife and slice.

The room is still as I start cutting away.

Soon, deep cathartic sobs ring out in the dank cell as I

cut through the bindings to remove Ethan's restraints. Travis's chants turn into, "Thankyouthankyouthankyou."

My girl is not feeling the love. She's already out the door and on the move. She's nobody's fool.

I'll support you, whatever you need, she said. What a load of shit.

I free Ethan and then move to Travis, putting my knife under his chin.

"You wait until we're gone," I tell him, applying pressure to the blade. "Then you get your brother some help."

He nods so vigorously, it looks like it hurts.

"I was not here." I begin cutting through his restraints. "Becca was not here. Remember, we got to you once. We can do it again."

More nods.

"You belong in jail, you piece of crap," I say, cutting a little more carelessly than I need to. "But sinking you would sink us too. So I guess we're stuck with each other."

"If that's how it has to be, I can live with it," Travis says.

"We have no choice," I say before running out that door for the very last time.

———

We'd never tell; we couldn't. We'd become forever connected … forever bound to our secrets. I trusted that Travis would never say a word. He had too much to lose. I'm sure Becca could've found a way out, but she didn't try.

That night was the last time I saw her.

Cass was right: Becca's parents sent her away to get help. They really did seem like they loved her, now that I think about it, but I'd only seen what she wanted me to see when I was under her spell. I believed everyone was against her.

It's crazy, but I miss her every day.

At least our secrets are safe.

Though there is still one thing that bothers me. I wish I could talk to Becca about it. It's Ethan. Sometimes when that last night plays on the screen behind my eyelids, I see that expression he had on his face. That movement I swear I saw out of the corner of my eye when he was unconscious.

That fleeting moment is burned into my brain.

I wonder. What did Ethan really see while we had him tied up?

Hear?

What does he know? Was he passed out that entire time, or was he listening, scheming? Were we being played?

I, for one, hope we never find out.

50

So that's how it ends? After all the work, all the planning, all the things that could've gone wrong, it was Johnny who threw it all to hell.

That's why you can't trust people.

People are unpredictable.

"Becca." A short, plump nurse reads my name from her chart. I call her *Teacup*. "Time for your meds."

I walk over to her, place the pills in my mouth, and take a sip of water under her watchful eye. My little show works every time.

But I won't say *where* I've been putting those pills. A girl needs her secrets.

"Thank you," I say before giving her an authentic smile— not Dad's passed-down grimace. A real one; the kind people like. *Teacup* returns it.

See, I'm learning.

I follow the crowd back to our rooms for naptime. Of course, that's not what I'm doing in my room. I have far too much on my mind to sleep; far too much to organize and get ready. I thought my plans for Travis and Ethan were elaborate. That was nothing compared to what I'm working on next.

It's okay, though. I have plenty of time.

Maris Ehlers Photography

About the Author

Dawn Klehr is the author of the young adult thrillers *The Cutting Room Floor* and *If You Wrong Us*.

She began her career in TV news, and though she's been on both sides of the camera, she prefers to lurk behind the lens. Mostly she loves to get lost in stories—in film, in the theater, or on the page—and is a sucker for both the sinister and the sappy. She's currently channeling her dark side as she works on her next book.

Dawn lives in the Twin Cities with her funny husband, adorable son, and naughty dog. Visit her online at dawnklehr books.com.

Don't miss Dawn Klehr's
Flux debut, *The Cutting Room Floor*.

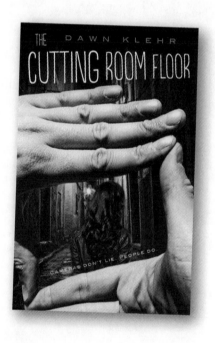